CHARLEY PARKER

THE ADVENTURES
OF A POST SERVICE
DECORATED SOLDIER

by
Dave Horn

Gotham Books

30 N Gould St.
Ste. 20820, Sheridan, WY 82801
https://gothambooksinc.com/

Phone: 1 (307) 464-7800

© 2024 *Dave Horn*. All rights reserved.

No part of this book may be reproduced, stored in a retrieval system, or transmitted by any means without the written permission of the author.

Published by Gotham Books (April 17, 2024)

ISBN: 979-8-88775-807-7 (P)
ISBN: 979-8-88775-808-4 (E)

Because of the dynamic nature of the Internet, any web addresses or links contained in this book may have changed since publication and may no longer be valid.

The views expressed in this work are solely those of the author and do not necessarily reflect the views of the publisher, and the publisher hereby disclaims any responsibility for them.

Charley Parker had been in the army all his adult life, he joined the green Howards at 17 years old and retired at 55 years old as a Sergeant. He had seen and done it all, Ireland the Falkland's Iraq Afghanistan. He had experienced war in all its horror he had shot and killed countless men carried a corporal with a foot almost torn off cradled a young 20-year-old as he died with his intestines bulging out of a horrific cut from the casing of a IED, holding them in with a blood-soaked towel.

His superiors accepted him as an unbelievable lucky soldier, he had not received a scratch in spite of being always in the front line his stoic attitude had protected him from the physiological problems suffered by so many front-line servicemen. His conscience was clear, if a man deserved to die and he came across Charlies line of sight Charlie killed him without a single hesitation.

Before he became a platoon sergeant he was trained as a sniper, a job he was excellent at, in fact one of the best the regiment had ever had with over 60 confirmed terrorist kills.

TABLE OF CONTENTS

CHAPTER ONE 1
CHAPTER TWO 2
CHAPTER THREE 4
CHAPTER FOUR 6
CHAPTER FIVE 9
CHAPTER SIX 11
CHAPTER SEVEN 14
CHAPTER EIGHT 17
CHAPTER NINE 18
CHAPTER TEN 24
CHAPTER ELEVEN 25
CHAPTER TWELVE 27
CHAPTER THIRTEEN 30
CHAPTER FOURTEEN 34
CHAPTER FIFTEEN 36
CHAPTER SIXTEEN 38
CHAPTER SEVENTEEN 45
CHAPTER EIGHTEEN 48
CHAPTER NINETEEN 51
CHAPTER TWENTY 53
CHAPTER TWENTY-ONE 57
CHAPTER TWENTY-TWO 59
CHAPTER TWENTY-THREE 67
CHAPTER TWENTY-FOUR 70
CHAPTER TWENTY-FIVE 78

CHAPTER ONE

Harry Tindall was 54 years old, in 6 months he would be 55 and entitled to retire on a pension of £50,000 per year; 80% of his present £60,000 salary as Assistant Chief Constable of Yorkshire. The pension was index linked and for life! After 36 years in the force Harry had risen to his present position by sheer hard work and dedication to the job. He had started as a raw recruit in Leeds in 1958 when all that was required for qualifications was the ability to add up to 20, sign your signature and have a clean record. Harry had a clean record when he started but for 36 years he had been a bent copper.

Royston Smith was 55 years old and was now at the very top of his chosen career. Roy, like Harry, had made it to the top with hard work and dedication to the job.

Harry and Royston lived next door to each other in Farquason Street, Chapel Town, Leeds, a long street of brown brick-built terrace houses with earth toilets in the small grubby back yards. They were both sharp and intelligent boys; George Tindall, Harry's dad, had been a plate layer on the railway. Royston's dad, who had immigrated to Leeds from London's East End, had died when Roy was only 8. Both boys had left Mrs. Lighthouses class together at the age of 15.

CHAPTER TWO

Pure batter ran through the veins of Arthur Bancroft. The fish and chip shop empire consisted of 3 shops which sold for the unheard of price of £50,000 in 1956 to the Morelli Bros Ice Cream Kings. With this generous sum, Arthur moved from the flat above his first chip shop in Cockcroft Ave and bought a nice brick bungalow in Swillington, invested a tidy sum with the Leeds Mutual Building Society and started 'Leeds Chip Shop Supplies'; everything for the chippie.

Roy and Harry started together with Arthur as gofers. Roy's father, Ron, had something few people had in those days – a driving license. Royston Smith was on the license and Roy had kept hold of this battered red license.

Harry and Roy worked for Arthur for 2 years; petty crime provided both excitement and petty cash for the boys until on 5th November 1958, Bonfire night – The Great Guy Fawkes Celebration, Arthur Bancroft died in a huge fire which engulfed 'Leeds Chip Shop Supplies'. The entire office and warehouse were burnt to the ground, and this is where Arthur's body was found; burnt beyond recognition. It was thought that a stray rocket had entered the building through a skylight and started the fire by igniting 1½ tons of beef dripping, 70 boxes in total fueled the flames sending black smoke and orange flames into the cold November skies. With their employer dead and their employment opportunity finished, Harry and Roy went separate ways.

One week later Harry became a police constable at Methley Police Station. A cynical person would have laughed loud and long at this but on closer appraisal what better place for a wolf in sheep's clothing that in the fold!

Roy started in business for himself. Although starting on his own he made few mistakes; concentrating on commercial premises it didn't take long to increase his initial stake of £1,500 to nearly £5,000 with his first investment being the Old Embassy Cinema in Eland Road. He did this by using Eli Cohen, son of Marty, who was a newly qualified solicitor to handle his negotiations. He paid £3,000 officially but £1,000 in cash to Sammy Brockley who had inherited the cinema, along with other houses, from his dad.

The cinema had been closed and was boarded shut. Upon obtaining the keys Roy went into the gloomy old building to exam his purchase. There were faded posters lining the foyer – Clark Gable, Errol Flynn and the likes stared out at him. At the back of the huge screen there were several small offices which had, at some time previously, been the dressing rooms for the days when the embassy was a live theatre. He walked into the largest and sat in a spindle backed elm farmhouse chair and placed his feet on the old desk. Written in blue crayon on the cream wall opposite him was the words 'smile if you fucked Mary Simpson this week, she has the pox'. Roy smiled, he knew Mary Simpson, but he certainly hadn't fucked her.

CHAPTER THREE

Harry drummed his fingers on his desk and stared at the calendar on the office wall reflecting on what he knew.

The small shop at the corner of Wallace Terrace and High Street, Manchester was his very first investment. He bought the shop with its small 2-bedroom flat above for £1,500 straight cash from Mr. McGee. McGee's Cousin Savoy Pillay registered the deeds and carried out the paperwork. Harry didn't like Manchester but his investments had to be far from home.

Mrs. Weston came with the shop; she had worked for McGee. Filoo and 5 children moved out of the tiny flat immediately, but it took Mrs. Weston 6 months to smother the smell of curry and kids.

It was arranged that at 8pm on the first Friday of every month Mr. Tindall would arrive at the shop and proceed up the small back stairs into the smaller of the two bedrooms where, on the desk, the monthly accounts would be laid out for his inspection together with that week's takings and the bank receipts for the remainder of the month's takings. Harry checked it with only a cursory glance, ruled a line across the book and put the takings in his pocket before entering the little living room to have tea with Mrs. Weston.

The very first time after making this arrangement, Harry arrived to find Mrs. Weston so upset she was almost hysterical. Eventually calming her down, he got the story from her.

During that afternoon, two men had entered the shop. One man had gone behind the counter while the other closed and locked the door, turning the open/closed sign to closed and pulling down the green blind. Mrs. Weston was terrified, she had never seen these men before and this couldn't be good. The man behind the counter put his face close to hers and said "We have come for the payment."

"What payment?" she managed to stammer.

"The payment you make every week from now on like the Baboon did, you stupid bitch!" With this he pressed the sale button on the old till; with a ping the till draw opened and the man emptied the contents – £48:25.6d. He flicked the sixpence back into the draw and said "We will be back next Friday for your insurance premium." As they left the shop he pushed a pile of tins over and they fell to the floor with a horrible clatter further terrorizing Mrs. Weston.

Harry looked at her tear stained face, she was shaking like a leaf. He poured her a cup of tea and placed in her shaking hands.

"What are you going to do?" she asked "They just took the money and said they would come back every Friday."

"Mrs. Weston, just relax and leave the problem to me, a man will be here about lunchtime next Friday to take care of this. His name is Daz."

CHAPTER FOUR

Daz joined the Elland Road Corporation three weeks after it was formed; he had come from Wakefield. Currently he was working as a bouncer for 'Fat Hymie' at the Regency Dance Hall. Roy stood at the door and watched Daz work; he had a raw presence. He was six foot tall, large boned and all his features were big; his hands, his knuckles, ears, nose, teeth; he was just…what? Roy couldn't define it.

Fat Hymie stuck his florid face around the door marked 'staff only' and shouted "Hey dummy, get into the karzie there's a ruckus going on – quickly!"

Daz looked slowly from Fat Hymie to the crowds of people pushing and jostling to get to the entry ticket office and then back to Fat Hymie; "Fuck you Fatso" he said in a grating heavy Wakefield voice as he passed Roy on he way out of the premises. Roy caught his eye as he went passed and asked "Do you want another job?"

"Doing what?" snapped Daz.

Roy took out a £10 note and placed it in his top pocket "An executive," he said, "I have just the position for you." He took out a card and gave it to Daz; it read 'The Elland Road Corporation'. Daz turned the card over but there was nothing on it.

"Do you know the Old Embassy Cinema in Elland Road?"

Daz nodded.

"I'll see you there tomorrow at 9:00am. Have a haircut and get a new suit."

Dennis Laughlin had been nicknamed Daz – short for Dazzle; why it was Dazzle, no-one knew but he was not called anything but Daz. He was completely controlled universal savagery; he was absolutely the most lethal person Roy had ever come across; his vitality and strength were pure prodigious. Although not of great intelligence, he was a unique person with a strange quality which seemed almost incongruous. After 36 years with Roy as his enforcer he was very wealthy; still capable of great savagery but very dignified. He was 100% loyal to Roy; his very existence centered on Royston Smith.

Daz caught the 8:15am train to Manchester on Friday as instructed. Dressed in a black lounge suit with a blue shirt, wearing large black sunglasses, his appearance caused concern to the general public, but the most striking feature was his shaved head – 35 years ago this was almost never seen. Written in small print just above the folds of skin on his neck, where it met the swell of his head was tattooed: made in Wakefield.

Black, expensive, kid gloves on each hand covered his specially designed and made aluminum knuckle dusters.

From the train he caught a taxi to Wallace Terrace. He stepped from the taxi and looked up and down the road, brick terraced houses lined either side; where it met the main road, he entered the doorway of the small shop. The doorbell pinged as he entered and Mrs. Weston looked at him uneasily even though she was expecting him. A huge grin spread across his face, his large white teeth shone, and the left front tooth was gold capped. Silently he took himself through the shop to behind the curtain, out of sight from the public. At 5:00pm the two men entered the shop and exactly as before, one man closed and locked the door while the other went behind the counter, grinning at Mrs. Weston, and pressed the sale button on the till. At this time Daz stepped from behind the curtain landing a punch into his kidneys with such a force that it ruptured his spleen. It severely damaged both kidneys and sprung three ribs from his spine. The force of the blow was so great that the man thought he had been hit by a car. He fell to the floor in a crumpled heap.

The other man, who had been standing watch at the front door holding onto the green blind, heard the drop, saw Daz and tried to open the door. It was too late; Daz placed one hand on the counter and vaulted it in one movement landing beside the man before he had any chance of leaving. He placed a hand on the man's throat, his thumb under the jaw line, and squeezing lifted him off the floor completely. The man's eyes were bulged; he could feel the strength and power of the bald man in front of him through this one hand.

"Who do you work for?" he heard the rasping voice ask "Who?"

The man couldn't answer any more quickly "Big Mustapha and Sam Organdy."

"Where?" the rasp came again.

"The Blue Lantern." he replied as best he could. The muscular hand increased the pressure before suddenly releasing him from the grip.

Daz walked behind the counter and stepped over the first man "Get him out of here now!" he said.

CHAPTER FIVE

The Blue Lantern was a seedy night club and drinking den off the Bull Ring. A large paunchy Arab man was stationed at the front door.

Daz walked straight up to him and pointedly said "Mustapha and Sam".

After looking him up and down the Arab decided it might be best just to answer this man, he didn't need the trouble. "In the office." he said.

Daz put his face so close to the Arab's that he could smell his breath, and although he was eating mints they were only partially working, his breath was still bad. "This is private Saboo" he said, "you can either take action now or fuck off for a while." The Arab shrugged and walked out into the street.

Daz walked to the office door, it was locked, and he knocked and waited. A little window in the door slid open "Yes?" asked a voice.

"A message for Mustapha and Sam" Daz said.

"Yes?" again queried the voice but Daz did not answer. After a few moments the door was opened with the security chain still on – Daz kicked it open, entered and closed the door behind him.

The hospital removed the pencil from Sam Organdy's hand but the poison took 6 months to subside in his arm; Big Mustapha lost an eye and several teeth. Mrs. Weston never saw the two men again in her shop, or any other problem people for that matter.

CHAPTER SIX

The Tollington family was headed by a wizened ancient woman called Pirie. Three sons and a daughter ran the largest amusement organization in Britain. Pirie Tollington was the last remnant of the Gypsy culture in the north of England. She lived in a huge chrome plated caravan on the small country estate 'Covingdon Priory' owned by her eldest son Parsley. People fell about with laughter when the family names first became prominent as the lucrative empire grew in status. Parsley, Oregano and Mint were the names of the three boys. Of course, the girl's name was Rosemary. The brains rested with Rosemary, the muscle with Oregano and Parsley while Mint just went along for the ride.

Their unusual names were no handicap to them; their weekly take in cash was over £20,000 when a man's wage averaged at £8 per week. The brightly colored carousels and roundabouts with flags and pennants fluttered all over Yorkshire, pinball machines, one armed bandits, grab a soft toy and shuv machines poured money in like a never-ending stream to the Tollington coffers.

Rosemary invested, their money in many lucrative ventures. Having been educated at St Mary's Convent in York and London Polytechnic.

She was very sharp and ran the financial side with great expertise. However, all the cash proceeds had to pass through Pirie's hands to impart the 'fluence'. So, every month when approaching £100,000 the money was packed into little plastic bags and ferried across to the chrome plated caravan to have the fluence passed on to it.

Carlo Morelli, the spoilt son of one of the Morelli Ice Cream Kings, and Peter Maharty broke into Covingdon Priory one Friday night making a hell of a mess and stealing bits and pieces. The constable arrived at the huge oak door and pulled the handle; on a wire somewhere inside a peel of bells sent the pigeons fluttering from the Central Bell Tower. Parsley Tollington and his bimbo answered the door, it was Saturday morning.

"I have come to investigate the break in Sir." he explained as Parsley opened the door and managing to keep a straight face as he remembered the family names.

Parsley was a showman through and through. "Step this way Constable." he said bowing with a flourish before ushering the policeman into the brick paved entrance courtyard. "May I introduce the lovely Belinda." he said turning to the peroxide headed young lady.

The constable turned to view this apparition who giggled and held out her hand while bending forward. The policeman had the ridiculous thought that she meant for him to kiss the proffered hand; he smothered the thought and said "Hello Lovely."

They were standing in the huge reception room looking through the bay windows to the terraced gardens which ran down to an ornamental lake.

The policeman could see what at first could not believe were Muscovy ducks in the garden on the bright green lawns at the side of the lake. These ugly creatures seemed to fit in well. Across the lake, in the middle of the meadow amongst the milk maids and buttercups stood a large chrome plated caravan. From its black chimney with a serrated cowl belched black smoke which trailed away across the meadow leaving a path which seemed unable to rise and started to fall back to the green meadow before dissipating. He was fascinated with the setting before him and had lost his train of thought when a strange sound ding dong, ding dong, came across the meadow; it was the silly little jingle of the Morelli Ice Cream van. He looked to Parsley for an explanation.

Parsley smiled "Every month Ma has to see the takings, so we bring it in an ice-cream van – nobody would ever suspect what it was carrying." The constable looked back at the green and yellow Ford van now parked beside the chrome plated caravan. "No-one would ever guess." he heard Parsley say again.

Rosemary had married Peter Morelli, thus joining the amusement empire to the ice cream kings. Peter arranged a different van every month for the delivery to Covingdon.

CHAPTER SEVEN

Roy's first big job became known as the 'Bridlington Ice Cream Job'. It was one of the major robberies in Yorkshire's history although the police were never truly aware of the amount involved.

Roy, Jimmy the Bean, Daz and the twins sat in the shelter with the rain beating down relentlessly around them. All five sat slouched on the wooden slats with their legs outstretched. For a while nobody spoke. For three days now they had been in Bridlington, and it was the end of the month.

Jimmy broke the silence "Jesus, these Gypsies may be called poofter names, but they are clever little bastards. How the hell do we spot which van is the one we want when there are dozens flying about all over the place? If I have to eat another Morelli super snow drift, I will go mad."

Roy took the match from his mouth "We may have missed this month's drop now but I have an idea that will put us in the park for next month. The money must be placed in one of the stainless-steel lift-out ice cream boxes; so in whichever van they use, they obviously won't be selling ice cream from it."

"But…." Jimmy tried to interrupt but Roy continued.

"This one van won't need its compressor running for its fridge."

"How does that help us?" questioned one of the twins.

"Well, the compressor runs on a separate motor. The exhaust for this motor is a small grill on the side of the truck. When the compressor is running you can see the fumes coming out of this grill. We need to look for the truck that is not running its compressor. We have learnt today that there are 5 vans that run out on the Scarborough Road and only 1 of these went down Kelston Road.

If that's the one, we are after we can't wait until it has turned into Kelston, or we will be sitting ducks; there is no other road out of there. We must stop the truck on Scarborough Road.

****

The brightly colored little van sped along Scarborough Road with Freddy happily whistling behind the wheel. He only did it 3 or 4 times a year but he enjoyed the Saturday delivery to Covingdon. It made a nice change to his routine. What Freddy didn't realize as he was enjoying his drive was that his little van, without its compressor running, had been spotted by some keen eyes. Apart from Freddy, the road was empty until a Standard white pennant pulled out of a side road and followed the ice cream van. The twins Lawrence and Clarence, nicknamed Lol and Clal, sat in the back of the van with Jimmy the Bean driving. Clal was holding a small Winchester gallery gun across his knees. They had worked for the circus and although Lol was good at shooting, Clal was deadly.

The ice cream van was now slowing down, stuck behind a Bedford truck, slower and slower it went. Freddy was about to switch on the 'Ding Dong' of the truck to give it the hurry up. "Now, hit it!" said Jimmy. Clal leant out the window; crack went the little gun as it jumped the short cartridge out causing only a little report. The ice cream van veered to the left and came to a halt at the kerbsibe; it had a flat rear left tyre.

"Damn!" said Freddy. He jumped out of the van to inspect the tyre when it dawned on him what was happening. From the front, a large man with a rubber ape mask gout out of the Bedford van and two identical 'rolly polly' men dressed as clowns got out of the Standard from behind. Freddy was no hero; he stood quite still and left them to their business. It was all over in 2 or 3 minutes flat. The ice cream box disappeared into the Bedford van and the van and car drove away. Freddy walked slowly to the telephone box at Kelston Road. This was a call he wasn't looking forward to.

****

Parsley Tollington was purple, he walked purposefully backwards and forwards in front of Peter Morelli's desk. "No friggin' insurance, no friggin' insurance!!" he repeated furiously "Why would you have no insurance?"

"Because," Peter said slowly "we are only insured to carry friggin' ice cream not thousands of pounds. Jesus, what did you expect?"

"Jesus alright, Ma has threatened to put a curse on you and me and all your friggin' ice cream vans.

CHAPTER EIGHT

Jimmy Stack was an alcoholic who happened to own a scrap yard at Canal Street. It was a ½ acre site of wrecked cars, pipe, channel bars and all manner of steel scrap. He sold the whole concern to The Elland Road Corp and had agreed to stay on and manage the business. What a laugh that was but it gave both parties what they wanted; Jimmy stayed in the office and drank all day and Roy had his laundry.

Phosphor bronze scrap sold for £600/ton, gunmetal for £800/ton. Roy bought 65ton of phosphor bronze from Cohen's for £35,750. Cohen's accepted half in cash and half by cheque. It took 3 days for the whole team to change the coins into notes at banks all over Bradford and Huddersfield.

Roy sold the scrap to the Union Corporation for £42,000 but asked for 2 separate letters of credit in US$. 1 was to be for $4,200 made in the favour of H Tindall and payable to Oporto Bank of Portugal in Lisboan and the other for the balance made in favour to The Elland Road Corp.

2 weeks after the great Bridlington ice cream robbery Jimmy the Bean deposited $4,200 into the account of H Tindall in Oporto Bank National, Lisboan.

CHAPTER NINE

Clal took the tiny brass shell and placed it between his lips, it was smooth and cold and he could taste the lubricant used on the die during its mass production. He gently eased open the breech on the Winchester and carefully placed the tiny bullet into the breech. The twins were sitting in the van in the empty milk depot across the road from the huge engineering works 'Octavious Dickenson and Sons Co. Ltd. The edge of the car park was fringed with bushes and the van was almost invisible from the road.

Lol glanced at his H Samuel Everight wristwatch "It's late." he started to say.

"No, here it comes." said Clal.

'Ding, ding, ding' the railway crossing gates started to close – it was 2:25pm.

The black steamer chugged across the road behind the red and white crossing gates. 'Whoo whoo' the steam produced a shrill whistle scream. At the first whistle Clal raised the rifle, at the second he fired. The small 25g lead bullet, travelling at 1,500ft/second hit the Osram bulb and a fine silver rain of glass fragments fell onto a pile of 1/2" steel plates piled up beside the building. The muted crack of the low velocity bullet was lost in the scream of the whistle from the steamer.

Fred Credland was employed by Octavious Dickenson and Sons Co. Ltd. as night watchman. He had retired from the railways 10 years earlier, and the small sum paid to him kept him very comfortable. 7 nights a week, with the exception of when emergency work contracts were being carried out, Fred sat in the small hut near the entrance spending most of the time dozing. At 10:00pm he roused himself and shuffled off to the little café on the corner of Railway Street just 50 yards from the factory entrance. Every night was the same he roused himself and walked to the cafe to order his bacon and egg buttie – a large round bread cake, fried on both sides in bacon fat, a large piece of bacon and a runny egg together with a half pint chipped mug of tea with 6 spoonful's of sugar. The whole process took approximately 25 minutes from his leaving his seat to returning again. Nobody at Octavious Dickenson was aware of his actions; even if they had, nothing would have been done about it. Maurice Dickenson, grandson of Octavious, was now Managing Director of the company and was weak and ineffective. An army of manager's clerks and other staff were the ones that truly ran the company.

All this information, together with a hard drawn map of the offices, had come to Roy by the usually method. Pay day would be the 24th December and over £6,000 would be safely delivered to the company on Thursday 22nd December to be held in the large Barchester safe ready for the Christmas holiday pay and bonuses.

Daz was seated on a stool at the counter and Doris came to the other side of it from the little kitchen at the rear. Subconsciously her fingers went to the fading yellow bruise behind her left ear. At 10:30pm three weeks ago, she had walked passed Daz at the door on her way out of the Embassy Night Club with a drunken lout called Paddy. But around the corner Paddy had grabbed her by the shoulders and pushed her against the wall lifting her skirt and grabbing at her panties. "No, no" she said as she struggled to push him away.

"You bitch," Paddy said thickly "you are going to get it AND like it." With that he hit her hard behind the ear and again commenced to pull down her pants.

Daz had watched them leave while outside having a smoke; he could now hear a commotion and walked around the corner. Inside of Daz was a very potent trigger; his savagery was awful and he could, and did, inflict terrible injuries on those who prayed on the helpless and defenseless or even just the appealing. If you were lucky enough for him to be around you could rely on unbelievable chivalry. Hence, Doris was saved the indignity and pain of rape. Paddy was not so lucky. He was so shaken by his encounter that he returned to Ireland unrecognizable mentally.

Doris was just a simple girl who worked alone in the shop her parents owned. They lived in a flat above the shop but as her father was very sick, they rarely came downstairs. Daz had been into the café many times since the incident at the club but his presence had never lessened and Doris again caught her breath. "Coffee?" she asked.

"Yes please." Daz took off his dark glasses and looked deep into her eyes. "I need a favour." he said to her.

"Of course, anything." she replied.

Daz smiled "Are you alone at night here, say 10:00pm?"

Doris was puzzled "Yes, but why do you want to know, I don't get any trouble from anybody?"

"No, no." Daz said "Just after 10:00 each night, a night watchman comes in for a buttie." He looked at Doris and raised one eyebrow.

"Yes" she answered "every night."

The small café was empty and Daz moved his face close to Doris now. He knew that she would die rather than disappoint or betray him, and he did not need to involve her really. "Do you think you could keep him here for an extra 15 minutes or so, just delay his buttie?" he smiled.

Doris smiled back and moved closer to him "No problem." Somehow being asked this favour made her feel special inside. She didn't really care, but the thought had crossed her mind, why?

Fred looked at the large clock on the platform at the railway station beyond the yard; it was 9:55pm. He folded his paper, stood and carefully closed the door behind him and walked across the yard. He unlocked the large brass padlock on the chain to the double gate and returned the chain and replaced the padlock, but he did not fasten it. It looked secure and only a close examination would reveal that it was unlocked. As he disappeared around the corner, two figures emerged from the milk depot car park and ran toward the double gate.

"We have exactly 45 minutes." Daz told the shorter fat man with him. Charlie Davey was a locksmith; trained as an iron monger 30 years earlier; locks were his life. They had earned him 2 three year spells in Wakefield Jail. "It's open." Daz said and they went through carefully closing it behind them.

They quickly crossed to the office block; it was a huge brick building at the rear on a mezzanine level. Daz looked up at the flood light with its broken bulb; ordinarily the whole area was bathed in light but tonight it was dark and quiet. At the small landing at the top of the iron stairs, Charlie examined the Mortice lock "Easy peasy" he mumbled while Daz looked carefully around the yard – all was quiet. Charlie placed two little picks in the key hole and lifted the tumblers one at a time. He then placed a larger wire hook into the hole and slowly turned the lock until it slid open.

Inside, Daz produced a torch and shone it across the office to a door on the far side that lead to the accountant's office. They approached the door and Charlie turned the knob, this was too easy the door was unlocked. Across the room stood a huge safe; Charlie knelt beside it and giggled "ha, ha." It was a 3 lever combination lock mechanism; 2 forward, 1 back and 1 forward. He took a stethoscope from his pocket and placed the suction pad 6" above the brass wheel; spinning the wheel he listened carefully before moving the suction pad down about ½". Again he spun the wheel and inside the lock he could hear the levers freewheeling "Beautiful" he breathed. Daz looked at his watch; they had been inside 7 minutes now, 20 minutes to go to be safe.

Slowly Charlie turned the wheel clockwise; it took about 1½ turns before he heard the soft click as the first lever clicked into place. It only took another ¼ turn to get the second soft click. Now he reversed the wheel ½ turn anti-clockwise, another clicks. One to go, clockwise, slowly slowly, and then he heard the last soft click. "She's open" he said. Daz turned the bar and the rods moved out of the housings and the huge door swung open.

The money was stacked in £100 piles of 5's with rubber bands around them. Daz carefully placed them in the duffle bag.

Let's go, he said to Charlie and as he closed the safe door he spun the wheel. Now outside on the landing Daz told Charlie to lock the door behind them which he quickly did and they made their way to the milk depot with 5 minutes to spare.

Fred relocked the large padlock on the gate 10 minutes later as he made his way back to the shed. Looking up at the broken light he shook his head, "Bloody dark without that light" he said quietly to himself.

****

Roy knew that even though his men were aware of his enforcer days that the knowledge would not always prevent someone from sometimes either overspending or carelessly going outside their normal lifestyle. To combat this, all money was first laundered and only then allowed out, little by little. This had a double effect; it prevented problems arising from drunken sprees and also kept his men tied to him for their livelihood.

Roy counted out the money onto the table in his office "£6,500, exactly right eh?" he said to Daz.

"Yes boss" Daz replied.

Daz knew that his boss had connections but where and how this information came to him, Daz never did know but it certainly put them firmly in the lead. They even received information about other firms.

Roy opened a draw in his desk and brought out a folded piece of paper. Roy unfolded the hand drawn map. Faintly, in the middle, Roy could see the water mark imprinted into the paper and wondered if Daz had noticed it. Even if he had, would he deduce anything from it 'Metropolitan A Grade' probably not. He folded the map and placed it in his desk draw with 500 pounds.

CHAPTER TEN

The phone rang and the desk sergeant picked up the hand set; he grunted a couple of times before saying "OK, I'll get somebody there straight away."

"You'd better take Harry." he said to Detective Inspector John Powell as he hung up the phone "he was there a couple of weeks ago helping sort out their security."

CHAPTER ELEVEN

Charlie Parker, to describe him at first seems easy. A short grey haired medium sized, although slightly fat, non-descript grandfather wearing a brown shabby cardigan buttoned up the front, baggy brown cords and a faded plaid shirt. On closer inspection one would see highly polished black boots, bright piercing blue eyes and wrists above his large hands that were unusually thick. In fact, if he had ever had handcuffs put on him, they would have struggled to close them. Above his wrists the forearms were very muscular and the biceps extending from them were in fact very large indeed. The covering layer of fat disguised the fact that Charlie was a very muscular man.

He had joined the army at 17 years old, coming from a council estate in Glasgow. For 25 years Charlie had exercised every day of his life and retired at the age of forty-two as a sergeant of the green Howards. He had seen action in Northern Ireland, Iraq, Afghanistan and Somalia there was nothing that Charlie had not seen in the way of depravity and man's cruelty. It was estimated that he had personally killed over 90 people. Married to Mary for 23 years, he had one son named John.

Retired now, Charlie was quite happy tending his passion for roses in their cottage garden. They had bought their cottage in Wetherby, north Yorkshire 15 years earlier and the garden itself ran down to the river. His pension was enough to live on happily. For 6 months after his retirement he and Mary enjoyed this lifestyle until events changed his circumstances and sent him back to his roots; many people would rue the day they came across that shabby middle aged man.

CHAPTER TWELVE

It was market day in Wetherby and Mary was shopping before waiting for Charlie to arrive at the square to pick her up. Two Hells Angels stood beside their Harleys in the square. One was a huge bearded giant covered in tattoos, the other was a smaller swarthy looking guy but equally tattooed. Mary stood near a stall and placed her shopping bags on the ground while she waited to be served.

As Charlie parked the car and got out he noticed the smaller of the Hells Angels walk up to Mary, lift her skirt and tug at her panties. Without hesitation Charlie ran towards them but seeing him approach the giant stood in Charlie's path. He placed his hand on Charlie's shoulder and said, "Leave it Grandad". Charlie hit him with the speed of a cobra strike just below his heart. The blow was so swift and violent the man's eyes opened wide; he knew he was in trouble; he felt his heart flutter and stall, Charlie's blow had stopped it beating. As he staggered Charlie struck again, this time hitting him just below his jaw and breaking it. The giant fell, spread eagled, onto the pavement.

The other man was still tugging at Mary's panties, oblivious to what had happened to his friend and what was now heading his way. Charlie hit him with the same savagery. This time he struck the man just below centre of his back squashing both kidneys. The pain was extraordinary. He tried to turn and face the man that had struck him but the blow had paralyzed him and he slumped to the ground.

Charlie went to Mary and hugged her, she was trembling. She was shocked but unharmed. By this time the local police had arrived. Statements were taken from Charlie and Mary as well as other people that had witnessed the incident. While the statements were taken, an ambulance had arrived and taken the two Hells Angels to hospital. Charlie and Mary were allowed to go home.

The next day Sgt Morris phoned Charlie's house and spoke to Mary. They were requested to head into the police station in connection with the previous day's incident.

On arrival they were taken to an interview room. It was a bare room, pale green in color with 3 chairs and a steel table with a leather top. Two police entered the room and identified themselves as Detective Inspector Oldfield and Sergeant Morris. They placed a tape in the recorder already positioned on the table and sat down.

"Interviewing commencing with Charles and Mary Parker in connection with the incident in Wetherby on 15 July 2009 at approximately 1:15pm. Can you please explain what happened?" asked the detective.

"Two men assaulted my wife and I stopped them". Charlie stated in a matter of fact voice.

"One man is dead and the other is on dialysis as his kidneys are so badly damaged" the detective stared at Charlie and raised an eyebrow. Charlie returned his gaze without further comment. "Did you consider the action you took to be justified?' continued the detective.

"You saw the men" Charles said "if I had asked them to stop do you think they would have complied? As I approached I was told to 'Leave it Grandad' and he placed his hand on my shoulder to stop me from approaching my wife and the other animal. I took the action I considered appropriate at the time. I only hit the first man twice and the other once".

The detective looked at the rumpled man sitting opposite him. "That may be the case but you stopped his heart. What we have to decide is whether this was deliberate or accidental?"

"I hit him with sufficient force to prevent him from taking any action against me. The fact that it killed him is unfortunate, but in the heat of the moment it is impossible to contemplate the consequences of such a blow. I needed to get past him to stop what was happening to Mary and he tried to prevent me. The same applies to the other man; he was assaulting my wife, in broad daylight, in front of several other people."

Detective Inspector Oldfield looked at the file in front of him "You were in the army for 25 years?"

"Yes."

"You have several commendations for bravery and you were awarded the George medal for extreme bravery under fire in Iraq." Charlie said nothing. "We have statements from several people who witnessed this incident involving your wife's assault and they all confirm your statement. Unfortunately, the Assistant Chief Constable is insisting we bring charges against you for using undue force." Again Charlie did not reply. He was then charged with using undue force causing death and physical damage. He was released on bail to appear in the Magistrate's Court in two weeks' time.

CHAPTER THIRTEEN

After returning home from the police station Charlie had immediately contacted his last commanding officer, Major Sandwort, and explained what had happened. "Leave it to me Charlie, we use a very good barrister in Leeds, I'll get him straight on it." Harvey Waterman was senior partner in Waterman Hemsworth Solicitors in Cross Gates, Leeds.

Mary and Charlie entered Wetherby Magistrate Court in the town centre. Mary sat in the body of the courtroom while Charlie proceeded to the front and sat with Harvey to the right of the room; the police prosecutor stood to the left. The magistrate entered the court and sat; they all sat down while the clerk passed the papers to the magistrate and announced "Case No. 586, Charles Parker charged with using undue force." Charlie and Harvey stood.

The magistrate read the papers before him. The purpose of the hearing was to decide whether there was sufficient evidence to proceed to trial. "On reviewing the evidence before me, I am satisfied that his case should proceed to trial. Therefore, it will be held at the Magistrates Court in Leeds at a date to be determined. Due notice will be given. Bail is to be continued" With that statement, court was adjourned.

Three months later, Charlie and Mary arrived at Leeds Magistrates Court. As before, Mary sat in the courtroom while Charlie stood beside Harvey at the front. Also in the courtroom were a number of bikers, obviously associates of the same biker's club as Douglas Johns and Gordon Smith.

The charges were read to the court; "How do you plead to the charges?"

"Not guilty." Charlie replied loud and clear.

The jury was sworn in; there were 5 women and 7 men. No objections were raised as each name was read out.

The prosecutor stood to make his case to the court "My Lord and members of the jury, this case is about the extreme action taken by the accused which resulted in the death of a Mr. Douglas Johns and severe injury to Mr. Gordon Smith on 15 July 2009. The prosecution maintains that this action was well in excess of that required at the time of the said incident. I have a written statement from Mr. Gordon Smith claiming that Mr. Douglas Johns was simply standing in the square at Wetherby when Mr. Parker approached him and hit him. He further states that Mrs. Parker's skirt blew up in the wind as he passed her and Mr. Parker proceeded to him and punched him also. Unfortunately, due to his severe disability, Mr. Smith is unable to testify in person.

The defense then stated its case. Harvey rose and acknowledged the judge. "Mr. Parker saw two bikers, one of whom stood 6' 4" tall and weight 150kg and another who was assaulting his wife Mary. As you will learn from a witness, this other Biker – Mr. Smith – pulled up Mrs. Parkers skirt and was attempting to pull down her pants. As Mr. Parker rushed up to help his wife, the giant of a biker – Mr. Johns – blocked his way and placed his hand on his shoulder attempting to stop Mr. Parker from reaching his wife. Mr. Parker took what he believed to be appropriate action and hit the man in order to get passed him. Unfortunately, this blow stopped Mr. John's heart. Although no defects were found in his organs at the autopsy who can say that this is normal; and the shock of being hit by a much smaller, seemingly old man, may have had some effect on his heart."

"Mr. Parker then proceeded to stop Mr. Johns assaulting his wife. He only hit this man once before going to comfort his wife. This account has been confirmed by three separate witnesses."

In summing up Jason, the prosecutor acknowledged that even though the Biker's statement denied any wrong doing, the reason they were in court today is the matter of one using excessive undue force.

Harvey addressed the court "My Lord and members of the Jury. You have heard today from witnesses that Mr. Parker indeed feared for the safety of his wife. You can all see how intimidating these people can be. Sgt Parker has served his country with honour. He is highly decorated for bravery and merely acted in the only way he knows how in order to protect his wife. We are becoming a nation of hostages to a weakened society that places more emphasis on the protection of these animals than on the safety of the public. This case has been a waste of public money; charges should never have been laid against Mr. Parker for protecting his own. Ladies and Gentlemen, send a message to these animals that we are sick and tired of justice being short changed and find Mr. Parker innocent of these ridiculous charges."

The jury took just 2 hours of deliberation before returning to the courtroom.

"Mr. Foreman, have you reached a verdict?" asked the Judge.

"We have your Honour." replied the Foreman.

"Do you find the defendant guilty or not guilty of these charges?"

"Not guilty, your Honour."

The Judge thanked the jury for their time, released them from duty and adjourned the court. "Mr. Parker, you are free to go."

Mary was waiting in her seat while Charlie shook hands with and thanked Harvey. The bikers rose and started to leave the courtroom but before they did a particularly large man with a huge beard and an eye patch bent down over Mary's shoulder and whispered 'You will be sorry" before grunting and joining the others exiting the room.

Charlie went to Mary and held out his hand "Let's go Petal." A large number of people had gathered outside the courtroom but at least the bikers had gone. They managed to push their way through the crowd and reach their car without incident. It was here that Mary told Charlie what the big biker had said to her. "We will take it a day at a time and deal with what comes our way." was Charlie's reply.

CHAPTER FOURTEEN

In 2003 in Kandahar Province, an armored vehicle moved slowly along the dirt road. Corporal Jimmy Kendrick was driving with Charlie sitting in the front left passenger seat and three other men riding in the rear. Ahead there was a bend in the road where stood a collection of remnants from what used to be several stone buildings. As they approached the rubble an improvised explosive blew right under the front off-side wheel crumpling the reinforced floor plates. A piece of this ripped metal plate sliced into Jimmy's right foot almost severing it at the ankle. The steering wheel slammed into Jimmy, breaking his arm. Charlie heard the clatter of an AK47's and the bullets buzzed through the vehicle killing one of the men in the back. Charlie quickly dropped onto the dirt, the two unharmed men from the back joining him. "Radio support." he barked "I'll get Jimmy." He approached the driver's side of the vehicle and quickly assessed Jimmy's condition.

"How are you doing Jimmy?"

"Not good." he replied "My foot's gone and my arm hurts like buggery."

All the time bullets pinged off the damaged vehicle. Lucky for them the Arabs were not marksman; they just pointed the weapons and pulled the trigger. Charlie reached into the vehicle, and being careful to grab is uninjured arm, he pulled him onto his shoulder. Grabbing his leg, he then hoisted Jimmy onto his shoulders and started running for cover. A bullet hit the ground and ricochet off the sole of his boot but another hit Jimmy in the thigh. "Let's go Charlie!" shouted Jimmy. Charlie stumbled his way to a small stone wall about 20metres from the vehicle and they both fell to the ground behind it for cover. Using a webbing strap Charlie applied it as a tourniquet to stem the flow of blood from the severed foot and gave Jimmy a handful of morphine tablets he had taken from the first aid pack. "Hang in there Jimmy, back up is on the way."

"Thanks Sarg, thanks Charlie." Shock had drained the colour completely from Jimmy's face now. Charlie patted his good shoulder and replied "You'll be OK."

Charlie unslung his Steyr and lined up on a small building about 75metres away. "Give 'em hell Sarg." Jimmy said. Through the scope Charlie could see 3 or 4 Arabs behind, and to the side, of a building firing at them with their AK47's. He lined up the first bearded head and squeezed the trigger; the head dropped as the bullet smacked into him. As he lined up and shot his second target the support vehicles arrived sending the last Arab scrambling to his feet running. Charlie took the shot which hit him in the centre of the back; he fell spread-eagled onto the desert sand. "Three from three, good shooting Sarg!" said Jimmy before he collapsed.

Charlie received the George Medal for his efforts. Unfortunately, though, Jimmy lost his foot and was discharged. He would be crippled for the rest of his life. He and Charlie remained firm friends. Charlie could count on Jimmy for anything; he was his savior.

CHAPTER FIFTEEN

It had been a few weeks now since the court case and things had gone back to normal.

At the back of Charlie's house was a large steel shed which he used for tinkering with all things mechanical. Over the years he had acquired a lot of machinery including lathes, milling, drilling machines, grinders, and polishers. Also, inside was a small steel room in which Charlie kept his collection of weapons. He had made quite a collection over the years, most of which were illegal and unregistered. As returning servicemen were not subjected to luggage inspections, Charlie had bought back all manner of guns and weaponry.

Charlie was in his workshop this day when he heard the rumble. As he came out of the garage to investigate he saw the first biker throw a bottle which crashed through the lounge window, trailing flames from the wick, and exploded. Another biker threw a second bottle that landed in the front bedroom before they powered away down the road. Charlie rushed into the house to be confronted by enormous flames started by the petrol. Running into the bedroom he found Mary crouching on the floor, her nightie was ablaze. Ignoring the debilitating heat, Charlie rushed to Mary and lifted her onto the bed, using the bedspread to smother the flames. Once the flames were out he stumbled outside onto the front lawn.

In the distance he could hear the sirens, obviously the neighbors had contacted the fire department. An ambulance arrived within minutes of the fire truck but it was too late. Charlie knelt, cradling Mary's head in his lap and holding her hand. She closed her eyes.

"Hang on Mary, just hang on." Charlie pleaded.

She squeezed his hand ever so lightly, and he tightened his grip as he looked into her pale face. She opened her eyes and whispered "I'm sorry Charlie, so sorry."

Charlie had many times held men as they were dying; he knew she was going. "Don't worry" he lied "you'll be OK." He held her as the light slowly went from her eyes and her hand went limp, she was gone.

Mary died principally from shock and burns. Inside Charlie, a small white hot spot burned to an incandescent heat.

The police interviewed Charlie and the neighbors but apart from the sound of motorbikes at the time of the fire, there was no other evidence.

As for the bikers questioned, they supplied alibis for each other

There was an inquest into the fire but nothing could be substantiated.

"Sorry Charlie." Detective Oldfield said.

Charlie had no response; he just stared and said nothing.

The house had been completely guttered and consequently demolished. Charlie received a $300,000 payout from the insurance company and used part of this to place a caravan on the now empty slab. He had work to do!!

CHAPTER SIXTEEN

Charlie missed Mary; she had left a large hole in his psyche which he filled with plans of retribution. He would destroy the bikie gang completely. He planned to kill every last one of them. He sank into his armchair to plan his campaign. He had no conscience whatsoever about killing 30 people, which is the number of bikers he estimated to be in the club. His main concern was to carry this out in complete secrecy. He would pick them off one by one.

The biker's headquarters was an industrial unit next to a car repair business. They called themselves the Devil's Disciples and this was painted over the doorway. They had been situated at Tex's home, their former leader, before being evicted. Tex was no longer their leader either; he had been killed by a revenge filled woman who believed he had killed her daughter.

Charlie drove a light blue Camry, quite inconspicuous and nondescript. He pulled into the B and Q's car park opposite the gang's headquarters in order to observe the layout of the grounds and the gang members' comings and goings. He could see an exit at the opposite end of the car park to the headquarters. There was an area to the right of the building which they used to park their bikes. From there they would walk to a small personal door to the left; to get there they had to walk across the front of the building. Situated at each end of the building were two huge floodlights that made the building look as if it was daylight at night. While sitting in the quite dark corner of the B and Q's car park he made the decision on how to take the first one out.

Charlie would need some help with this and he knew just the man to ask, Jimmy Kendrick. And so he called him.

"Jimmy, I need an alibi on Wednesday night."

"No problem Charlie, anything I can help you with?" Jimmy asked.

"No, this is strictly a one-man job. Can you come to my van at 6:00pm?"

"Of course Charlie, I'll be there."

And that was that; Charlie knew that no matter what, Jimmy would be there for him. It was 5 years since the bombing attack and Jimmy had just as much respect for Charlie today as he did then. Charlie knew that Jimmy would do anything for him. Even if he was tortured Jimmy would remain resolute in his support for Charlie.

****

It was Wednesday morning and Charlie was preparing for the night ahead and was currently at the local rifle range. He signed in as a visitor and hired a 222 rifle and set up 2 targets at a range of 75m. He placed the rifle on the bench with the bolt open and waited for the range master to walk by and check.

The bell rang and the range was declared open. Charlie loaded the bullets one at a time before taking his first shot; it was slightly high and off centre so he altered the scope down and to the left before taking his second shot; this was better, just one more adjustment. The remaining bullets entered the tiny black dot in the centre of the target.

He then reloaded the rifle and took aim at his second target; all 6 bullets would fit into a 50 cent piece at the centre of the tiny black dot. When he had finished he opened the gun and waited for the red light to flash and the range master to declare the range closed before going to collect his targets.

Charlie returned the rifle to the front office where the rifle master accepted it and noticed the targets in Charlie's hand. "Can I see that?" he asked.

Charlie handed him the target.

The man was clearly impressed "Where did you learn to shoot like that 'Old Timer'?" Charlie just smiled and shrugged. "Can I keep this?" he asked.

"Sure." said Charlie.

****

One of Charlie's favourite rifles was a Mauser Sniper specially adapted from a standard service rifle that fired a 7.35 bullet. It was fully customized with a specially polished action; the bolt pushed the bullet into the breech as if it was sliding on silk. Charlie had designed and made a special silencer; a huge fat cylinder filled with wire gauze, the noise it made was a soft splat.

That night Charlie positioned himself in the B and Q's darkened car park. Apart from the floodlights at the bikers' headquarters the whole estate was dark and silent. He had watched several bikers enter the building but he was waiting for a single man to enter on his own. It didn't matter to him which one it was. And then he heard it, the rumble of a single Harley as it entered the car park at the side of the building. A large man pushed down the support stand and swung his large frame from the bike. He was dressed in the usual leather and chains and had long hair and beard. Charlie opened his car door and rested his rifle on top of it as the man made his way across the front of the building. Through the scope he could clearly see the man who was now only about 6metres from the door. He had paused and was pulling a packet of cigarettes from his top pocket. He placed one in his mouth and reached into a pant pocket for a lighter. Charlie picked up his head in the scope and moved down slowly passed his ear to his neck where he could clearly see a spider web tattoo on his thick neck. He was aiming for his jugular as he wanted a through and through shot leaving less chance of investigations finding the bullet. As he centred the target on the centre of the web he gently caressed the trigger; 'splat' the solid point bullet pierced through the large vein in his neck and ricocheted off the concrete wall and landed 150metres away in the roadside gutter among the general roadside debris. The next rainfall would flush the spent bullet down the drain, lost forever. Being a solid point bullet it had passed through the man's neck leaving a hole that spurted a stream of blood under pressure which gradually slowed as the heart pumped out his life blood. He was dead within seconds. Nobody came, no sound was heard. Charlie unscrewed the silencer and placed it in a cardboard tube used to post drawings and paintings. The rifle slid into a compartment behind the rear armrest into the boot behind the side covering. Anyone glancing into the rear of the car would see nothing suspicious. As he left the car park he glanced again at the man laying motionlessly on the concrete in front of the bikers' headquarters. Half an hour or more had gone by before any members had left the club and discovered the body. By this time Charlie was having a beer with Jimmy.

****

Jimmy came from a small farming community and when his mother finally died he inherited a small 100acre farm at the edge of the North Yorkshire Moors about 45minutes drive from Wetherby. On the property was an old stone farmhouse and a couple of dilapidated buildings. Jimmy's army pension was enough for him to live on even if a bit frugally. When Charlie had first embarked on his mission he had approached Jimmy for help to find a new place for his weapons collection. Without hesitation Jimmy had offered his place.

"I don't want to compromise you." replied Charlie.

"What is that supposed to mean?" asked Jimmy.

"I don't want you to get into any trouble by hiding my guns and equipment."

"Fuck off" interrupted Jimmy "I'm only here because of you, of course you can hide them here. We'll just do a good job of hiding them, that's all."

Jimmy had a large, old half-timbered barn with some equally old farming equipment that would come in handy. They cleared a space and dug a 3m deep hole approximately 3m square taking the earth out into the field and spreading it with the front blade of the tractor. It only took about 2 weeks and the grass was growing through leaving no sign of the earth being tampered with. They then bought 1,500 concrete blocks and had them delivered together with 26 bags of cement and 5metres cubed of fine sand. They worked together concreting the floor of the hole and building 4 block walls to floor level of the barn. Across this they placed 3 oak beams that had at some time fallen and rolled across the barn. On top of this they constructed a floor with old boards to conceal the room. In the corner they made a 1metre square trapdoor directly above a ladder which was fixed to the block wall below. Once straw was strewn over the barn floor you couldn't even tell the room existed. To further protect it from discovery they made the area into what looked like a sheep pen with wooden hurdles. Charlie then moved his considerable armory into the room onto trestles and shelves they had constructed from old bits and pieces lying around the farm.

****

Detective Inspector Oldfield was standing beside the green coated lab pathologist in the mortuary looking down on the dead biker on the slab. "The shot landed just centre of the main artery to the brain, he would have been dead in seconds. I would say it was from a military rifle, probably a 7.35 solid point through and through.

"Detective Inspector Oldfield and Sergeant Morris were now interviewing about 10 of the bikers in their clubhouse. Each of the bikers was sitting silent and sullen; they didn't like dealing with the law. They had asked a few questions to no avail but would try once more.

"Who do you have problems with?" asked Detective Inspector Oldfield.

"We deal with our own problems." stated one of the members.

"Perhaps a rival gang?" pushed the detective. He was met by silence.

"OK Sgt, let's go, we aren't doing any good here?"

Outside the clubhouse he looked around. He was sure the shot must have come from the car park across the road. They crossed the road and inspected the area but there was nothing to indicate where the shot had come from. The coroner had estimated the time of death at approximately 11pm; B and Q would have been long closed by then but they went in to ask if anyone had seen anything. No one had.

On the drive back to the station Detective Inspector Oldfield suggested that perhaps they should get Mr. Charlie Parker in on the chance is was a payback. They had no other leads to follow.

Charlie had been expecting the police to call and agreed to go into the station. He sat in the same interview room, same chair and at the same table.

"Where were you on Wednesday night Mr. Parker?"

"I was with a friend, Jimmy, at his house from about 5 until 3 in the morning."

"Name?" demanded Dec. Ins. Oldfield to which Charlie gave him Jimmy's details.

"Do you own any weapons of any sort Mr. Parker?"

"No, I do not? What is this about?"

"Do you mind if we take a look around your house?"

"You know the house is gone. But you are welcome to look around wherever you like." Of course, they found nothing.

"I would also like you to come down to the station with me and be tested for gunshot residue – just to be sure, you understand."

Charlie opened his wallet and took out a receipt from the rifle range and handed it to Detective Inspector Oldfield. "This will show that I have."

"Of course it will." sighed the detective with a wry smile. "I'll check this out."

CHAPTER SEVENTEEN

For the next execution Charlie had chosen a 222; it was a German gun with a double barrel 12 bore and a 222 barrel in the middle at the top. He had taken this weapon off a dead Somali terrorist; who knows how he had obtained it but the gun was obviously a relic of the colonial days. Charlie had carefully restored the old gun to its former glory. It had no scope, but a leaf sight at the rear which lifted up to give incremental distances. The 222 gives a 75g bullet a trajectory of 2800ft/second with virtually no drop over the first 150m.

With careful observation from various places, Charlie had established regular routes taken by the bikers and The Devils Disciples were easily identified by the yellow tags on their shoulders. One of the frequent roads travelled was the M1 to the Leeds turn off. They liked this ride as they could ride 3 or 4 abreast, taking up 2 lanes of traffic, in complete contempt of other motorists. Charlie liked this route as it gave him ample opportunity to pick off his next target.

Charlie had chosen one of the bridges over the M1 that was only ever used for farm traffic, which was very rare. He parked at the Leeds end behind a screen of bushes. The bridge had one stone wall on either side; Charlie carried his 222 from the car in a badminton racket case. He didn't have to wait long; it was only about 10mins before he saw the bikers heading towards him.

There were 4 of them today riding arrogantly on their Harleys', legs spread out, boots pointing to the sky, completely oblivious to the other road users. Charlie set the hair trigger and waited until they had passed under the bridge before lining one of the bikers up. The 75g bullet hit the back of the helmet and penetrated straight through to the head; the biker never knew what hit him, he died immediately. His bike ran out of control, clipping the back of another bike sending the other rider hurtling under a semi-trailer that was coming the other way at 120k/hour. Two for the price of one thought Charlie as he smiled and placed the case in the boot of his car and slowly pulled away toward Aberford. An hour later he pulled up at Jimmy's place where he took the gun to the barn, being careful to strip and clean it before returning it back on the rack with the other guns.

****

"Bloody hell" said Detective Inspector Oldfield "someone's going to town on the bikers." He again looked down at the dead man.

"This one has been hit with a different kind of bullet to the last one." stated the pathologist. "The bullet passed through his head and was lodged in the front of the helmet. It appears to have come from a 222."

Detective Inspector Oldfield glanced at the slab next to the biker who had been shot. Here lay another body but this one was just one massive bruise. The pathologist caught his glance "He's quite a mess; a 75t rolling load will do that to you. All his organs have been completely crushed."

Walking to the car Detective Inspector Oldfield shared his thoughts with Sergeant Morris. "This is not a rival gang striking back, the weapons are too unique and it is too organized. This is someone who is not going to stop, someone with a personal grudge. I was sure it was Charlie Parker the first time and I'm just as confident of that now. His only alibi was from a friend and with no further evidence to tie him to the killings, what do you do? I know he doesn't look it but after going over his service record he is hard shrewd man with all the skills necessary to carry out these killings."

CHAPTER EIGHTEEN

Charlie had been following Joe and Billy; they were the debt collectors for the Devils Disciples'. They were the biggest and meanest looking of the whole chapter and easy to spot because of this. They enjoyed their reputation.

The skinny man they had been working on with their knuckle busters was finished. They had him pinned up against a rubbish bin "You have 24 hours to come up with the money" they said before letting him drop to the ground. Joe kicked him in the gut as he hit the concrete and they turned to leave the ally way.

"Hey, there's the old man who killed Douglas. Let's see how he goes against us." yelled Billy as they started toward Charlie. But as they advanced they realized too late that Charlie was holding a silenced 9mm which he raised and shot Joe straight in the mouth. He slumped to the ground.

"Whoa" said Billy "it's you that has been knocking us off."

Charlie fired his next shot, hitting Billy in the throat before he could say anymore. Blood was spurting from his neck and he went down coughing. Before he hit the ground, the old scruffy man had turned the corner and disappeared into the shopping centre. No one gave Charlie a second glance.

****

The pathologist had advised Detective Inspector Oldfield that the two bikers had been killed by a 9mm hand gun by the look of the bullets; both clean kills.

The badly injured skinny man had no information; he was unconscious when the police arrived.

"It would appear that he has caught them on the job. Judging by the knuckle busters on them, and the injuries to the other guy, the bikers must have been working him over when they were surprised." Detective Inspector Oldfield said to Sergeant Morris as they left the morgue. "How the hell does he track them is what I want to know?"

"They are not exactly invisible." answered the sergeant.

"Jesus," said Oldfield "he is going through the whole gang. Three separate incidents, three different weapons. We've got to stop him."

"Put a surveillance team on Parker." Detective Inspector Oldfield said when they returned to the station. "If it's him, we'll get something sooner or later."

Charlie had done covert surveillance in Ireland and was well aware what to look for and was expecting attention from the police. He noticed the car with two men parked about 100m down the road from his caravan. This did not affect Charlie's plans at all.

The police had also obtained two search warrants; one for Charlie's house and the other for Jimmy's farm. Although they didn't expect to find anything much in Charlie's caravan, they were hopeful the shed would hold something. Nothing, it was absolutely clean; there was nothing at all to incriminate Charlie. Next stop was to Jimmy's farm. They were in the barn and 6 sheep stared back at the officers from the corner "Corralled to lamb." explained Jimmy. A tiny newborn bleated in the corner and tottered to its mother to feed. Beneath their feet rested Charlie's armory, safe and secure. Again, nothing.

The team investigating the bikie murders, Detective Inspector Oldfield, Sergeant Morris together with Constables Alan Welsh and Sally Moffit were getting absolutely nowhere. Even the bikies wouldn't cooperate. They decided to look into other possibilities like a rival gang or someone other than Charlie Parker that may have a grudge against The Devils Disciples. Another violent gang known as The Gypsy Jokers overlapped into Disciples territory in Leeds and they had clashed in the past but just a few broken bones and bloody noses; nothing like the present situation. Still, it was worth looking at.

It had also now dawned on The Devils Disciples that they were under real threat. But as with the police, they had nothing to go on. The remaining 5 members of the committee sat in the clubhouse trying to make sense of their situation. "Did we start something when we fire bombed the old man's house? Think about how he killed Dougie, he's a dangerous bugger." Dangerous or not, they had enough arrogance to give them the kind of confidence they believed was enough to cope with this, "Let's rough him up and see what happens." They set about making a plan to raid his caravan late at night and take him by surprise.

CHAPTER NINETEEN

Charlie knew that sooner or later the bikies would put him in the frame; after all he had taken down 6 of their gang. He decided to lay low for a while and let the heat die down. In the meantime he would prepare himself for the expected.

Across the front of his property, Charlie had placed his trap. It was a thin wire entwined around pegs set close to the ground that ran to the caravan. Any disturbance to the wire would set off a buzzer in the caravan alerting Charlie to an intruder.

The bikies parked about 300m away and walked towards Charlie's property. As they approached the front fence one of the bikies had stood on the circuit sending a signal straight to the van. 'Ping' went the alarm alerting Charlie to the intruders. Charlie looked out of the window and saw them approaching. He dialed 999.

"Emergency Services, what is your emergency?" asked the operator.

"I am being attacked by Bikers." Charlie reported. "They have just entered my property and they look like they mean business."

After confirming his address Charlie was advised to keep out of sight until the emergency response team arrived.

Charlie lay on the floor of the van as the bikers fanned out and surrounded the van. From what he had seen, two appeared to be carrying shotguns and two others had hand guns. The first shotgun blast shattered the window before they all opened fire, bullets ripping through the van walls. To Charlie's surprise, the shooting stopped almost as quickly as it had started. The first response team had arrived and flooded the yard with spotlights stunning the bikies. The lighting revealed four heavily armed police directly around the van and more across the front of the property.

"Police, put down your weapons and drop to the ground."

Startled, one of the bikers turned and discharged his shotgun at police. He was shot in the chest. The others immediately threw down their weapons and knelt on the grass with their hands behind their heads, they had done this before.

****

The three surviving bikers from that night refused to talk to police and Charlie could not explain the attack to police. The subsequent police enquiry cleared Charlie of any wrongdoing and the three bikers were each convicted of weapons offences and sentenced to 3 years in jail.

"Jesus Christ!" exclaimed Detective Inspector Oldfield. "7 dead bikers in total and no tangible evidence as to who is responsible."

Charlie replanted his roses and considered his next move; he still had a lot to do but for the moment he would keep a low profile.

Six months passed without incident. The insurance company had paid Charlie $300,000 for his house. He didn't see the need to replace the house at this point; it would be empty without Mary. He did however replace the bullet filled caravan with a new one that he now called home.

CHAPTER TWENTY

Among Charlie's collection were RPG's (rocket propelled grenade). It was a favourite weapon of the Taliban; this grenade was dead accurate to 50m. It was this that Charlie thought he might use in his attempt to vamp up his revenge, it would make a nice mess of their clubhouse and 6 months had been enough time to allow things to cool down.

The RPG's, although accurate to 50m, were slightly less so once you took the range to 150m. They could be set to detonate at a set distance making them a lethal weapon indeed. This small and easy to transport weapon transported in two pieces and was no larger than a shotgun, although slightly bulkier. Using this weapon was much like a shotgun also; you rested it on your shoulder and took aim through the leaf sight. To use this weapon would be a big step for Charlie and he knew it would cause considerable damage.

Charlie wanted to be sure the clubhouse had as many members as possible inside when he made his move. Several days of observation had told him that Friday night was going to be his best time to attack; it was the one night they all seemed to come together. This observation period had also given him the chance to check where the clubhouse was most vulnerable. It was constructed from windowless concrete tilt up panel walls and it would appear the door was reinforced with a steel plate. As it was part of an industrial estate Charlie would have to be very careful not to cause damage to any other property or persons. The pallet making company next door would be particularly vulnerable.

Through his binoculars Charlie examined the whole building again. He just could not see how he could get the grenade inside the club house. As he examined the yard again where they parked their bikes he noticed the BBQ where they gathered on a Friday night – of course – an idea started to form in his mind as he studied the area closer. There was a gas bottle connected to the BBQ and two spare ones stood next to the nearby wall. Perfect, this was only a small area and he should be able to clean up the last 5 members' altogether. Next Friday, Friday the 13th, was going to be the final revenge on Devils Disciples. His vow to his wife Mary would be complete.

****

The day had arrived, Friday the 13th and the BBQ was well underway. Charlie, comfortable in his usual position waited. There were only 4 of the bikers around the BBQ laughing and joking, oblivious to what was about to happen. Charlie had bought a Swiss Steyr 222 rifle with a high powered scope; the expanding soft nose 18m bullets were already loaded and he gently chambered a round. Through the scope he sought the valve at the top of the gas bottle attached to the BBQ. He could see the steak and sausages sizzling away on the hot grill and flames leaping and dancing from the fat dripping onto the burning jets below. The yellow flames were dancing in the scope. With the crosshairs centred on the brass valve, Charlie's finger caressed the forward trigger. The rifle was equipped with a hair trigger system which meant you set the forward trigger first; once set a very slight touch on the second trigger was all it took to discharge the weapon; thus enabling a very accurate shot indeed. He now set the first trigger with a soft click before moving his finger to the second trigger. With the lightest touch the rifle discharged sending the little bullet at 2100ft/sec to the target. The valve disintegrated and blew the pressurized gas from the bottle with a huge explosion. In turn, this ignited one of the spare bottles with an equally large bang. The force was astonishing; two of the bikers were killed instantly. The other two weren't so lucky and writhed with pain for a few minutes before they too died.

Charlie was two kilometers away when the first police car arrived at the scene and at Jimmy's farm an hour later. The gun was cleaned and packed away on the racks beneath the sheep. They were sitting in the old kitchen with a bottle of whisky on the table between them. A fire burned and glowed in the blackened fireplace, the pear logs crackling softly.

The blue lights flashing through the kitchen window is what alerted them that the police had arrived and Jimmy went to open the kitchen door. Two constables and Detective Inspector Oldfield walked onto the porch and passed Jimmy into the kitchen.

"Where were you 2 hours ago Mr. Parker?" asked the Inspector.

"I've been here since 4:30 this afternoon" replied Charlie "what is it you think I've done this time?"

The Inspector looked to Jimmy who nodded his agreeance that Charlie had indeed been there since early that afternoon.

Detective Inspector Oldfield shrugged "At 8:30 tonight four people were killed at Highfield estate."

"And what does that have to do with me?" Charlie asked.

"They appear to be the last of the Devils Disciples motorcycle gang. You know them, members of the same club that attacked your wife?"

"They appear to be very unlucky people." said Charlie.

"Don't they just Mr. Parker."

"How did they die Inspector?" Charlie asked.

"We don't know exactly but it appears a gas bottle from the BBQ exploded."

****

The logs crackled and burned and the ash fell softly into the grate. Charlie swirled the brown liquid in his glass and finished it off before pouring himself another; about 25mm and the same for Jimmy.

He raised his glass "There you go Mary, it's finally over, they are all gone now. Rest easy my love wherever you are." His eyes half closed as he stared into the fire.

CHAPTER TWENTY-ONE

Taking into consideration the previous deaths in this particular biker's club membership, the police were convinced that the explosion was not an accident. But even with minute examination of all the evidence they had nothing to suggest foul play.

"If he is behind this" Oldfield said "he's either very lucky or very clever."

"I think lucky." said Sergeant Morris.

"Well his luck has held good for the whole gang Sergeant because we have nothing on him." The sergeant was halfway out the door when Oldfield questioned "Hey, when we checked Parker for gunshot residue in his last interview did we ever check with the rifle range that he had actually been there?"

"No sir, we did not. It seemed reasonable at the time that he would not lie about something so easy to check."

"Get out there now and see what they have to say." barked Oldfield.

Arriving at the rifle range Sergeant Morris indicated the date he was interested in and asked the man at the desk to check the register for a Mr. Charlie Parker. There it was, almost at the top of the page.

"Do you remember this man coming in that day?"

Looking at the bottom of the page, the man answered "No, I wasn't on that day. This page was signed off by Jack Preston."

"Is he here today?"

"Yep, he's range master today. Wait here."

The man went to Jack and told him there was a cop wanting to see him at the front office. "I'll take over here while you go talk to him."

Jack Preston proceeded to the office, "Sergeant, what can I do for you?"

Morris pointed to Charlie's name on the register "I don't suppose you remember this guy coming in here do you?"

Jack walked to the rear off the office and indicated a target pinned to the wall. On it was printed 'Free hand at 75 yards'. "This is what he shot, sure I remember him."

CHAPTER TWENTY-TWO

As he frequently did, Charlie was visiting Jimmy for a quiet drink. They were sitting in a comfortable silence gazing into the fire when the sound of an old fashioned phone rang. It was a loud jangling noise.

Jimmy got up from his chair and walked over to the phone "Hello."

"Hi Jimmy, it is Don Greyson." although he needn't have bothered identifying himself as Jimmy knew the voice well. They had served in the same squad in Afghanistan.

"Hi Don, long time since we last talked." said Jimmy.

"I know, too long. We should get together sometime and catch up." responded Don.

"So how are you anyway?" enquired Jimmy

"Yeah, good I suppose. Listen Jimmy, I need a favor. Are you still in touch with Charlie Parker?"

Jimmy laughed "Yes, he's actually here now drinking my single malt."

"Do you think I could speak with him?"

"Sure, hang on." Jimmy was puzzled and put the phone down on the small table in the passage and called Charlie to the phone. "It's Don Greyson." he said to Charlie and shrugged to show his confusion.

"Hey Don, how's things?" asked Charlie

"OK, I suppose." Don replied.

"You sure don't sound like things are OK Don, what's up?"

"Charlie, I've got big problems. Is there any chance we can meet somewhere so I can fill you in? You might be able to help." asked Don.

"You just tell me where and when Don." replied Charlie

"How about tomorrow at the coffee shop in Scargate market place, say about 11am?" asked Don.

"Sure Don, I can be there."

Charlie walked in and ordered a coffee. Don was already seated at a table next to the window waiting. He was a tall man with thinning hair and a prominent Adams apple. Charlie sat across from him "Hey Don, you don't look so good. What's going on?"

"Ah Charlie, I run a small delivery service in Leeds; it's not very big but enough to keep me busy. I've been paying protection money to the local crime mob known as Elland Road Firm, as everyone has to. Well business is down at the moment and I haven't been able to pay in a while. They have sent a man called Dazzle to see me; I don't mind telling you he's quite a scary bloke. If I don't pay them by the end of this week he'll be back and next time won't be to talk. You are the only person I could think of that could help me Charlie."

Charlie stared out the window across the street. He had quite enjoyed his little mission against the bikers and now that it was over he was at a bit of a loss as to what to do with himself. A smile crept across his face as he felt the excitement grow inside him. "OK Don, I'll help you. When will he be back?"

"He comes on a Friday and normally gets to my office about 6pm."

"I'll be there this Friday mate, don't worry." said Charlie.

"Thanks Charlie, really, I don't know how to thank you. He's an awful bloke." said Don, looking rather relieved after sharing his load with Charlie.

Charlie smiled remembering the worst of the bikers. "Don't worry Don I'll be there and we'll get this sorted."

****

On Friday afternoon Charlie arrived at Don's as promised and sat himself in the little office while he waited. He had sent Don out for a while.

It was 6:10pm when Dazzle walked in; he was 6'5", weighed 120kg and was a very solid man with a shaved head. Charlie could see a tattoo on his head but could not make out what it was. The sunglasses on his head added to his theatrical look. Dazzle looked at the shabby fat man "Where's Greyson?" he grunted.

"He's not here, he left me to talk with you today." said Charlie.

"Nothing to talk about; I just hope you have his money ready." Dazzle grunted as he stood a little taller.

"There is no money, not today, not ever. Mr. Greyson will not be paying anymore and you are going to leave now." Charlie stared blankly at Dazzle.

Dazzle's eyes flashed dangerously. "I don't know who you think you are but we'll see about that!" roared Dazzle as he advanced on Charlie.

Charlie stood and watched as the huge man advanced on him. Dazzle had expected Charlie to be intimidated but the scruffy little fat man stood his ground as Dazzle reached out a large hand to grab Charlie's jacket. Charlie ducked under the hand and jabbed a fist into his kidneys below his arm.

"Shit" exclaimed Dazzle as he exhaled and bent almost double over. It was like he had been hit with a telegraph pole. As he was going down Charlie hit him again, this time with his elbow just behind his ear. Poor Dazzle collapsed to the ground; he was completely out to it. By the time he began to regain his senses, his arms and legs were tied with cable ties and he had been hoisted up by a rope through his hand cuffs to a beam in the roof, his toes just touched the floor. His head and side ached very badly and he had been sick down the front of his shirt. Charlie was sitting on a chair facing him. It hadn't escaped Dazzle that there was obviously more to this little fat man than he had thought. How the hell had this little man been able to put him in such a position; never had he been humiliated like this in his entire criminal history. He wasn't exactly scared but it would be reasonable to say the Dazzle was concerned. He shook his head and grunted, he was having difficulty collecting his thoughts.

"Now" said Charlie smiling wryly "we are going to have that little talk."

"I have just finished off a complete gang of bikers." Dazzle's eyes widened with surprise, he had heard of the Wetherby bikie gang murders. "You pose no threat to me at all. From now on you will leave the Greyson business alone and if you or any of your organization has any further contact with him or his staff, today will feel like a tea party compared to what you will experience if I have to come back. Are we clear on that?" Dazzle nodded and the pain in his head worsened.

Charlie took out an old fashioned scout knife from his pocket and opened the blade. For a moment Dazzle panicked before Charlie cut his restraints and watched him almost collapse to the ground. Stumbling, he made his way out of the office and onto the street. There was a black Buick parked at the curb with a bald man sitting in the driver's seat. As Dazzle reached for the door he looked back at Charlie standing in the doorway; his hard face grimaced with pain as he climbed into the back of the car before it drove away.

"I think Don that will be the last you will hear from them." winked Charlie. "But you keep in touch." he said before turning to leave.

"Thank you, Charlie."

****

Three days later Dazzle was sitting in a leather arm chair opposite Royston Smith, the CEO of the Elland Road Corporation – the biggest crime syndicate in Leeds. What a sight Daz was, half of his face was a large dark bruise.

"You're looking good today." Royston said with a grin.

"Ha, ha." said Daz as he leant to the right and lifted his shirt to reveal a heavily strapped chest. But you could still see the yellow and purple bruising from his armpit to his waist.

"Three broken ribs and a fractured skull." whistled Royston.

"Yeah, I had to tell the hospital that I fell during a clubbing outing." On reflection Dazzle still could not believe such a scruffy looking, little, fat middle aged man could do so much damage. "I have to admit, he took me off guard. And I'll tell you another thing; I don't want to meet him again. We should keep well away from Greyson. Roy, if you are going after him you can leave me out of it. He is a one man wrecking ball."

After Daz left his office Royston sat and thought. Daz had been with him right from the very start and never before failed him in any way, no matter what was asked of him. It was hard to comprehend that Daz was truly intimidated by some old man and his attitude shocked him. That couldn't stop Royston though, he had come this far and would not be put off by one man, even if Daz was. He decided that he would get the twins to slow him up. But first he had to find out who he is.

Royston Smith was a very close friend of the Assistant Chief Constable of the Yorkshire Police Force. He had known Harry Tindall since they were very young and just starting out in life, but one chose the life of crime and the other followed the law. Fortunately for Royston, Harry was easily persuaded and Royston had been paying him for years for otherwise hard to come by information. Harry wasn't alone though. Royston had influenced several other policemen over the years. Jim Broadbent, a Detective Inspector stationed at Roundbay, was another.

Jim's mobile phone vibrated in his pocket and he pulled it out and checked the screen. "Hey Roy, what's doing?" he asked.

"Jim, I want to know who is leading the biker murders investigations, what can you tell me?"

"That would be Detective Inspector Oldfield." replied Jim.

"Mmm, I don't know him. Who is in his team?"

"I'm sure you know Sergeant Morris."

"Sure do, that's all I need for now. Thanks Jim." Royston terminated the call.

Roy's next call was to Fred Morris. "Hey Fred Roy here."

"Hello Roy." Fred said nervously.

"How they hanging?" chirped Roy.

"Yeah I'm OK Roy. What can I do for you?" he asked tentatively.

Roy told Fred he was chasing information about the biker murders, in particular if they had any suspects. Fred considered this for a moment and though of the envelopes he had received in the past from Royston containing a large amount of cash.

"We have a suspect but we can't get any evidence to tie him to it." said Fred.

"OK Fred, give me his name."

"A chap called Charlie Parker. He was charged with killing one of the bikers and putting another in hospital before all the murders happened but was released due to lack of evidence. He is still our prime suspect for the rest of them but we have nothing to go on." said Fred.

"Mmm, I remember that now. Thanks Fred." Roy said before hanging up.

The library is a wealth of information. It is here that Roy read all the Yorkshire Post articles on the biker murders and Charlie Parker. It gave detailed information on the trial, subsequent acquittal and Charlie's military record; interesting reading indeed.

Armed with this information it was time to call on Lol & Clal, the twins.

CHAPTER TWENTY-THREE

The twins had been given their instructions from Royston and they were now on the job; this was the third day they had been following Charlie trying to pick the best time and place to ambush him. They had followed him to the supermarket and watched him park his Toyota before entering the store.

They parked their Ford and waited for him to leave the store. When Charlie appeared at the store exit with his groceries they fired up the old Ford and maneuvered to a better position to start following him.

They could see the Toyota but Charlie had disappeared. "Where the fuck is he?" Lol said as he scanned the car park looking for him.

'Shit' half a brick had smashed through the passenger side window and a hand had grabbed hold of Clal by the throat pulling him from the car. Charlie threw Clal to the ground placing his foot on his throat and then pointed a silenced gun directly at Lol "Get out of the car and lay flat on the ground next to your friend." he said in a menacing voice. He scanned the car park but there was no-one anywhere near them.

The twins lay side by side on the ground; Charlie's foot still firmly placed on Clals' throat. "You two aren't very bright are you?" said Charlie with a smile on his face. "Now, who sent you to follow me? Was it that fool with the tattoo on his head? I warned him what would happen if we crossed paths again."

"No" said Lol "it was the boss."

"I don't have time for games. Who is the boss?" demanded Charlie as he put a shot into the tarmac to the side of Lol's head. The gravel shattered and hit him in the face; there may have been no sound but the effect was deafening.

"Royston Smith." Lol shouted "Royston Smith, that's who sent us."

"And exactly where would I find this Royston Smith?" asked Charlie.

"At the old embassy cinema complex in Elland Road, shit man, give us a break!" cried Lol.

"You tell him to expect me." said Charlie "And if either of you move in the next 5 minutes I will shoot you both." Charlie glanced into the old Ford and saw a guitar case on the back seat of the car. He pulled it out and opened it. Inside was lovely 22 Winchester Gallery Gun; he hadn't seen one these since the old fashioned shooting arcades back in the 50's. It would make a nice addition to his collection and he placed the guitar case in the boot of his car before driving away leaving the twin's face down in the car park wondering if he was still there or not.

The twins had returned to Royston and now sat on the table defeated "Jesus Roy, Daz was right. This man is not to be messed with. He caught us fair and square, he even took Clal's 22." Now Roy was worried also, two of his prize assets had been busted.

Charlie walked up to the entrance and through the front door leading into the newly refurbished cinema. Dazzle was standing at the rear of the room and saw him enter; his chest still hurt and he had a constant headache since there encounter so when Charlie approached and asked "Where is he?" Daz immediately turned and led Charlie up the stairs and turned left to face a door marked

'Private'. Daz turned the handle, opened the door and stood to one side allowing Charlie to walk right into Royston's office.

As Charlie scanned the room he noticed the fancy leather chairs, antique tables and huge elliptical desk which a tall skinny man was sitting behind. As Charlie approached the desk the skinny man looked up, a little startled, and said "Charlie Parker I presume?"

"You presumed correctly." said Charlie as he leant across the table. Thinking he was about to shake hands, Roy extended his hand. Instead Charlie took his own hand and hit him with a round house smack so hard it nearly took off his head; tears appeared in his eyes and the red stain spread over his face.

"The next time I run into you will be the last." stated Charlie as Royston gently rubbed his cheek. And with that Charlie turned and walked out. Dazzle just stood there and watched him leave. It was quite a while before anyone spoke.

Royston broke the silence "Jesus Daz, I wish that man was on our team."

"A bit late for that I'm afraid." said Dazzle in a shocked voice "Who would have thought a few days ago that this could happen, eh boss? I did warn you."

Roy rubbed his smarting face "I did not come this far to let a scruffy old man walk over me." he said sulkily.

"Boss, I think you need to chalk this up to experience and move on, he's too dangerous to provoke any further."

"You might be right Dazzle." pondered Royston "We'll have to find another way."

CHAPTER TWENTY-FOUR

Harry sat at a desk in his study at home. "What do you want me to do Roy?" he asked.

"I don't care, if you can't get him for the bikers, fit him up for something else. You're the Assistance Chief for fuck sake. Just do something." flared Roy.

The Assistance Chief Constable had gathered his group and was now leaning his considerable weight on the murder team. "This is the second time he has avoided the law! I want him charged! If you don't have the evidence the GET IT!!" he demanded, with the emphasis on the get it.

"Jesus boss!" exclaimed Sergeant Morris. "Does he expect us to fit him up?"

DCI Oldfield looked at the incident board thoughtfully. "It certainly sounded like that." he said.

"Sorry Sarg, you know me, I won't go down that track. But we aren't getting anywhere as it stands so let's start again and see if we missed anything." said Fred Morris. "So DCI Oldfield, where do we start?"

"Well a gun that matches with ballistics or a witness would be a good place, of which we have neither."

"We have searched his place and that of his alibi and came up with nothing. Do you want us to go back again?" Sergeant Morris asked.

"No if we didn't find anything the first time I don't believe another search will reveal anything, he's too clever." replied Oldfield.

"If he is our man why can't we pin anything on him? There's no evidence and surveillance didn't turn anything up either. In spite of the big fella's opinion, maybe it's not Parker. What is it about Charlie Parker that has him so motivated to pin this on him anyway? And don't you find it odd that this is the only case in a long time that he has shown any interest in at all? The more I think about it the odder it seems."

About a week later Fred Morris was in DCI Oldfield's office. "Peter, I have been thinking about this Charlie Parker business. We still have nothing and that Pratt Chief Tindall has been on us a couple of times this week. And now I've just had a phone call from Royston Smith asking about Charlie Parker."

Peter looked up quizzically "Why would he be phoning you about Parker?"

Fred knew that Roy would not reveal that he was bent under any circumstances; it would not be in his best interests to do so, so he explained "He is married to my wife's sister and we run into each other from time to time at family do's. Anyway, something doesn't feel right so I've been checking up on Tindall and found that he and Smith grew up together in Chapel Town. Do you think that Smith is somehow driving this?"

"That is interesting." pondered DCI Oldfield. "If he is, you are heading into very dangerous territory with this. You will need to be very careful Fred. Roy's top enforcer was badly injured a couple of weeks ago by a reportedly aging man. This man was a very capable animal himself so whoever did clean him up must have been good." He hesitated before asking "Do you think it could have been Parker? Let's face it, he proved his worth with the bikers, look what he did to them."

Fred considered this for a moment "Maybe that is why Smith is involved with this. But it doesn't explain how he can use Tindall." Thinking for a moment before continuing he said "Unless he has something on him."

"Jesus Fred! We are getting in really deep here now suggesting that the Assistant Chief Constable is linked to a major crime figure like Smith. If we are going to pursue this we'll have to tread very carefully indeed." said Peter with a worried expression.

"Leave this to me Peter. It's probably best you pretend to know nothing about this." replied Sergeant Fred Morris before leaving Oldfield's office.

Albert Bentley was a retired Detective Sergeant who now spent his days working as a private eye. He had worked with Fred Morris previously and they now sat in the Red Lion ready to discuss his next job with Fred.

"Albert" said Fred "I have another job for you but it has to be discreet."

Albert raised his eyebrows with curiosity but willing to listen as he owed Fred Morris for various bits of information he had supplied Albert over the years. "What is it you need?" he asked Fred.

"A good house man" was the reply.

Albert smiled "I'm listening."

"I need a hard copy of telephone records that I can't request officially so they'll need to be taken from the premises." stated Fred.

"That doesn't sound too difficult." smiled Albert "What is the address?"

He gave Albert the address along with a warning "Be very careful on this one. He's a big man with a lot of power and could prove very dangerous."

"Who is it 'The Pope'?" joked Albert.

"No" replied Fred "but close."

Albert enlisted the help of 'Bobbie the cat'. He was extraordinary at what he did. He scaled the drain pipe to a window on the first floor and 5 minutes later was in the downstairs office rifling through all the files. He found the phone bills and took photos on his mobile phone of the previous 12 months records as he had been requested. In less than 30 minutes we were back down the drain pipe and away. He returned to Albert who loaded the pictures onto his computer to print for Fred. It was then that he saw the name on the phone account and nearly choked "Fuck me" he exclaimed "what have you got me into Fred?"

Meeting again at the pub, Albert handed the photos over to Fred. "What were you thinking Fred? You can keep me out of this from now on. You are paddling into rough waters here." he said.

Fred laughed "That is why I picked you to get the records for me, I can trust you Albert. Thanks for this, I won't forget it; I owe you."

Back in his office, Sergeant Fred Morris looked up the yellow pages for the Elland Road Corporation and then checked this against the photos of the phone bill in front of him. And there it was once, sometimes twice a week every week over the last 12 months. He cut the name off the top of the photos and took his finding to Detective Inspector Oldfield.

"Oh Fuck!" exclaimed Oldfield. "Where on earth did you get these?"

"Never mind that Peter, look at the number highlighted in pink. That's Royston Smith's number and he has been calling Tindall weekly for as far back as these records go."

"Suspicious yes, but not conclusive proof that he is bent." said Oldfield.

"So, what do we do now then? Turn it over to Internal Investigation Department?"

"Fuck knows I'll have to think about this before I make any decisions. I don't mind telling you, I wish I knew nothing about all of this."

They were interrupted by the phone "DCI Oldfield" said Peter as he answered.

Fred could hear the agitated voice on the other end and was trying to listen in.

"Tindall?" he asked as Oldfield put the phone back in the cradle.

"Yep Tindall, he rang yesterday too and the day before. Smith must be leaning on him hard. Well that's it, there is only one way to go, we'll have to turn this in." said Oldfield.

"Do you want me to do it?" asked Fred.

"No, I'll do it tomorrow."

Secretly Fred was pleased as he didn't have the stomach to go Ethical Command and he hoped to keep himself away from the shit what would come down if Tindall was as bent as he suspected.

The offices for Ethical Command were located on the 15th floor of the police headquarters in The Headrow in Leeds. A phone call in the morning brought an immediate response "30 minutes, my office!" demanded Inkpen. George Inkpen and Stanley Bunbury were both Detective Inspectors of large commanding frames and impassive expressionless faces. They were waiting in Inkpen's office when Peter knocked on the door. He entered and sat in the chair indicated to him. Once the introductions were out of the way and Peter agreed he was ready to go Inkpen pressed the record button.

"Detective Inspectors' George Inkpen and Stanley Bunbury interviewing Detective Inspector Peter Oldfield commencing at 9:30am 15th January 2012. OK Peter, let's hear it." said Inkpen.

Taking a deep breath Peter began. He started with details pertaining to Charlie Parker and the full extent of their subsequent enquiries. This was followed by the intervention of Assistance Chief Superintendent Tindall before he finished with itemized phone bill.

"How did you come across these phone records?" asked Bunbury.

"At this stage I cannot reveal that. What I can tell you is that the highlighted number that appears repeatedly on this bill is from a well-known local crime syndicate. It is Royston Smith's personal number."

"Is there any possibility that this is an informer from with the syndicate?"

"No sir. As I said, this is Smith's personal number. He runs a very tight and successful operation. His crew is 100% loyal to him. We have not been able to pin anything on him ever." said Oldfield.

"That's an interesting choice of words DI 'pin something on him'."

"To be clear, I'm saying we have not been able to prove any illegal activity against Royston Smith over the years that he has been around." Oldfield corrected himself.

"These are very serious allegations DI Oldfield" said Bunbury leaning back in his chair.

"Yes they are. So what do you want me to do from here?" asked Oldfield.

"For now do nothing. Leave us go over this information and decide the best course of action. In the meantime keep up your probing of Mr. Parker and see if you can make a connection to Royston Smith and or Tindall without raising any flags." DI Peter Oldfield was dismissed.

Once he had returned to his office Peter called for Sgt Morris to give him an update on what had taken place.

"Jesus Fred this is going to be one hell of a blood bath. It's not often an Assistant Chief Constable finds himself under investigation. Who knows where this will lead?"

Fred sat silently looking into his lap with a worried expression on his face. It was getting close to him now.

Oldfield had noticed is expression and was surprised he had nothing to say "Is there something you aren't telling me?" he asked Fred.

"Nah, nothing for you to worry about Peter." replied Fred without raising his eyes from his lap.

"Oh no Fred, don't tell me you're involved? There will be blood if you are."

"He's paid for girls in the past, and a few bob as well. But I've never given him anything I swear. I think he wanted to keep me in reserve." pleaded Fred.

"You dopey bastard!" said Peter surprised at what he just heard. Fred remained silent. "OK" Peter continued, "We'll have to see what we can do to keep you out of it. As long as Smith doesn't break, you should be alright. But in the mean time for Christ sake don't contact him or answer any of his phone calls."

CHAPTER TWENTY-FIVE

The photocopy machine on the 15th floor was starting to grind. Marian Bloomfield was busy printing the past 20 years of telephone records and personal records for Harry Tindall since his entrance into the force to the present time. It was quite impressive reading; his record was unseeingly spotless and he had huge number of arrests, some of them involving the largest takedowns known to Leeds. But with each of his cases being carefully investigated, remarkably one thing kept appearing as a common denominator in each of them. Every case solved by Tindall had been a direct result of an anonymous tip off from an unknown informant. George Inkpen addressed his team stating that the telephone records they had obtained showed a disturbing trend; Assistant Chief Tindall's arrests were compared to that of the telephone records of Royston Smith. It was obvious now they knew what they were looking for, before nearly all of his busts there were calls recorded as being received from Royston Smith.

Royston and Dazzle were sitting in Roy's office. Physically, Daz was recovering well but psychologically he had taken a real battering. He had become quite withdrawn and Roy was not sure he would ever return to normal.

Jimmy had been asking around for information. Roy was concerned that things appeared to be unusually quiet at the moment. Jimmy knocked on Roy's door.

"What is it Jimmy?" asked Roy not sure that he wanted to know after seeing the sheepish look on Jimmy's face.

"I've been checking things out liked you asked boss and it doesn't look good. The word getting around is that things are shaky in the police force Gov."

"And exactly what does shaky mean?" quizzed Roy.

"A big investigation boss, right the way to the top brass they say." squirmed Jimmy.

"Oh Fuck!" exclaimed Royston. "Not now. We've had 36 good years. Not now."

Daz looked to Jimmy "What about the old guy, have you heard anything on him?".

Jimmy shook his head "Nobody knows anything, he's a complete mystery."

"Believe me, he's still around, I can feel it." said Royston softly. "I am beginning to wish I'd never laid eyes on him. You were right Daz, he's completely bad news and we shouldn't have poked him."

Simultaneous search warrants were served on Harry Tindall's home and the offices of the Elland Road Corporation. The Assistant Chief Constable was in his office; the details of the raid had been kept from him.

Harry Tindall had been careful and could have very nearly gotten away with everything by claiming the phone calls were informant's tips but for the file that had been found at the Elland Road Offices for the Oporto National Bank. The Oporto bank was located in Lisbon, Portugal and records showed that over a 36-year period over $150,000 had been deposited into an account bearing the name of H Tindall. Together with that and a copy of a single deposit slip in Harry's desk draw was enough, he was cooked.

Harry Tindall was charged with corruption and Royston Smith was charged with bribery of a policeman. The evidence was overwhelming and Barristers' for both parties advised their respective clients to plead guilty. In doing so they received a reduced sentence. Assistant Chief Constable received a 20-year jail term and Royston Smith a 10-year sentence. The Elland Road Corporation was finished.

Charlie read the newspapers with a certain relish. The pressure had gone off him as the corruption investigation had taken precedence. For the next 4 months at least Charlie could get on with his life, he would continue the plans for building his new home, tending to his roses and visiting Jimmy.

4 months after the corruption investigations Charlie opened his letter box and took out his mail, among the various advertising pamphlets was a light blue envelope plain without a sender's address in a spidery hand writing it read C Parker Sgnt 15 Cragg St Wetherby Nth Yorkshire.

Charlie sat in his wooden garden bench seat and turned the envelope over in his hand with his thumb he tore open the letter he pulled out the flimsy letter inside puzzled he opened the single folded sheet of paper it was written in the same spidery hand writing as the envelope it read.

Dear Mr. Parker I am sorry to approach you like this but I am at my wits end what to do and my beloved diseased husband Col Cuthbert Pearce told me just before he died that that when he was gone, you were the only man he could think of if I ever needed help was you.

Before he died my husband and I were battling against a huge company.

Charley placed the letter back in the envelope in his mind he went back 30 years to the parade ground at Richmond Yorkshire and a tall stringy man with a prominent Adams apple and a large hook nose Colonel Cuthbert Pearce.

corporal Charles Parker stood to attention in from of him "err um" Colonel Pearse cleared his throat corporal Parker I am pleased to present you with this medal as recognition of your obvious prowess as a sniper in this regiment the highest score ever achieved we are proud of you well done.

That was the only personal meeting Charley ever had with Col Pearse but obviously the old boy had followed his career in the Howards.

As charley had nothing on he decided to follow up on the request he had received. A quick phone call to records and he had the address he arrived at the small neat cottage a week later in the village of Wittersly.

He walked up the path to the front door admiring the roses in the small front garden, a tiny grey haired old lady answered his knock on the front door looking down at her bright blue eyes twinkled in the wrinkled old face sergeant parker I presume she said.

Charley smiled he held out his hand "Mrs. Pearse" he said she grasped his hand with both of hers her hands were soft yet quite vibrant Please call me Milly.

I am so pleased you came from what my husband told me I knew you would come in come in she leads him into the small lounge and told him to sit in the chintzy arm chair one of as pair Charley sat down and looked around the room a heavy oak beam across the middle with smaller beams running from each side at one side was a heavy polished mahogany side board with several photographs in silver frames on it amazingly one showed charley receiving his snipers medal.

She saw him looking at the photos and they both smiled at each other.

Would you like a cup of tea she said or something stronger!

No tea is fine Charley replied no sugar just a dash of milk please she seemed very happy to see him and stepped with a sprightly step into the kitchen fifteen minutes later she returned with a tray with a tea pot, two cups, a china jug of milk and a plate of scones with jam and cream.

That looks lovely thankyou now what can I do for you she looked at him with her bright blue eyes.

Well she said 5 years ago well my Cuthbert had been retired from the army for a few years he was offered a directorship principally I think for his rank and name on the board to increase the look on the companies manifesto the company Centenary construction had just been listed on the stock exchange and had tendered and won a huge dam on the Medway river in Kent.

Everything went well for the first 4 years Cuthbert went to shareholders meeting once a year and that was his only involvement for which he was paid 250 pounds.

A year ago a large collapse of the dam wall caused huge damage and the company was placed in liquidation We received this letter a few weeks later she gave Charley a document from Boarse and Penfold liquidation lawyers.

The letter stated the situation of Centenary constructions financial position with debts of one point eight million pounds and that as a director Cuthbert could be held responsible for a portion of the debts She looked a Charley as he read the letter.

With a quaver in her voice she said I think that letter caused his massive heart attack which killed him.

But that wasn't the end of it she continued 2 weeks ago three men came to the house they said they were from Thunderstruck debt collectors representing Heaver earthmoving who were owed 250000 pounds from Centenary constructions and they were visiting all the directors to collect a share of the debt my husband's share they said was fifty thousand pounds and they would give me three weeks to get the money.

Our only asset is this house and my only income is my service widow's pension which allows me to live comfortably but I have no way of raising the money without selling this house.

A small tear appeared in her right eye and grew then ran down her wrinkled cheek.

Sorry she said taking a small-flowered hanky from her skirt pocket she wiped her face and dabbed her eyes.

She looked at Charley they are due to return today she said in a small shaky voice.

Charley stood and put his arm around her shoulders well it good timing I came today then isn't it.

Oh dear she said I am so sorry to involve you in this don't worry replied Charley I have dealt with bullies before let's enjoy these beautiful scones.

About an hour later there was a loud knock on the cottage door Milly left the lounge and went to the door Three men stood on the porch two were normal well-dressed men in dark suits the third was much bigger with a shaved head also in a dark suit and sunglasses Charley turned and examined the men standing there the big man was obviously the muscle.

Please come in Milly said they came into the lounge the big man had to stoop to get through the door.

They ignored charley and one of the men addressed Milly have you got our money granny he growled I am sorry Milly said shaking No I could not raise that.

The big man spoke that's a pity he said looks like we will need to show you how important it is to pay up.

Charley stood up is that so he said and what does that mean he addressed the big man who took off his sunglasses.

I don't know who you are Grandad but I suggest you stay out of this or you will get hurt.

Is that right replied Charley, he had walked up to the big man and was close the man looked surprised and clenched a large fist what happened next was so fast it took the two normal men by surprise in an instant Charlies head went back and delivered a perfect head butt on the big mans' nose.

Like puppet with the strings cut the man collapsed and sprawled on the lounge floor Charley looked at the other two who appeared to be too shocked to move now get this gentleman out of here.

Gathering their wits they rushed over but the man was completely unconscious they struggled to lift him eventually one holding his shoulders the other his feet they took him outside.

Charley followed them out as they bundled him into the back seat of the car parked in front of the cottage.

If you come back again he told them there will not be one of you left to drive.

Charley went back inside Milly was on her knees cleaning the blood off the carpet he bent down and helped her up don't do that he said and hugged her get it professionally cleaned and give me the bill.

Oh dear Charley thank you but what if they return I doubt they will but what they are doing is illegal so if they return just ring 999 and tell the police.

I will see too it they never bother you again get the carpet cleaned and I will call and pick up the bill the company will pay for it I guarantee.

Back at the farm Charley looked up the address of Thunderstruck debt collectors the address was listed as Grosvenor terrace Hunslett Leeds.

Three weeks later Milly phoned and Charley arrived at her cottage how are you he asked much better she said last time you were here I was so shocked I didn't thank you properly thank you so much my poor Cuthbert was spot on when he told me you were to be relied on come in.

Tea and scones yes please Charley replied, but I am so worried about paying you Milly said.

Don't even think about it I like this kind of problem it keeps me young she gave him the bill.

Instant cleaning for 155 pounds I will get this back for you said Charley.

Grosvenor terrace was a back lane in industrial Hunslett old industrial buildings renovated and converted to business offices.

Thunderstruck debt collecting was at no 6 double glass doors which opened when Charley pressed the red button on the right hand side.

Inside the reception was opulent with quality paintings on the walls and a rich thick pile carpet on the floor.

Charley walked up to the large polished timber desk the young girl looked up yes she said can I help you could I speak to accounts please.

Can you tell me what this is about? she asked sweetly I have a bill here answered Charley.

Perhaps you should speak to Mr. Gowlett the general manager she said good idea said Charley smiling at the young girl just a moment she said.

Oh Mr. Gowlett there is a man in reception who I think you should talk to.

Ok send him up.

Charley stepped out of the elevator on the second floor along the corridor an extremely fat man with a red face stood at the door come in he said and offered Charley a chair.

How can I help you? The man said.

Three weeks ago three of your men turned up at a cottage in Wittersley and demanded money with menaces.

The man's face hardened I had to remonstrate with one of them and he made a mess of the carpet this is the cleaning bill.

You have a bloody nerve turning up here after what you did to one of my polite collectors Charley stood up and placed the bill on his desk the man pressed a button under his desk and within 5 seconds the door opened and two burley men came in.

This gentle man is leaving please show him out he said the two men came together to Charley who stood up they each took an arm but quickly realized this was no elderly grandfather the muscular arms told a different story.

A grip on anything has a weak point where the thumb and first finger meet in this case the could not meet leaving a considerably gap Charley used this applied pressure and broke both grips.

With his arms free he hit the first man fair and square in the balls he collapsed the second man was so shocked he hadn't moved Charley hit him just below his ear breaking his jaw and he fell to the floor beside the first man.

The fat man's face was now purple and he spluttered how dare you he roared Charley walked up to his desk and with his finger jabbed the invoice you get this paid today fat boy or I will be back and the next time it will be you needing an ambulance.

He looked down at the two men one completely unconscious the other still writhing about holding his wedding tackle.

Charley walked to the lift and past the lunch room the big man was sat at the table the bruises now fading but still yellow as he saw Charley he rose you caught me by surprise he growled Charley walked into the room there were two other men sitting let's see how good you are when I am ready.

You are a bloody fool said Charley.

Hold his arms boys he said before they could rise Charley hit the first with a cupped hand on his ear bursting his ear drum he slumped back in his seat screeching with the pain the second man just sat there staring at his colleague the big man came at Charley with two raised fists.

You are a fool said Charley oh yes said the big man and swung a hay maker Charley ducked as the huge fist fast his head he caught it and pulled the big man lost his balance and fell over a chair rising clumsily yes I will show you he approached Charley warily this time he reached out and hugged Charley hoping for a bear hug Charley kneed him hard in the balls once again the big man fell to the floor

Charley put a boot on his neck and bent down the next time I see you friend I will put you in a wheelchair for the rest of your life do you understand the big man grunted but fully convinced.

The other man was still sitting at the table staring at the carnage.

As charley walked out he spoke to the man please tell your fat boss to pay the invoice and forget Mrs. Pearse or he will have no staff left OK the man nodded.

Instant cleaning confirmed to Charley the were paid the same afternoon.

It was six months later after quite a few trips to Wittersley to assure Milly it was over that his phone rang.

Sgt. Parker the voice said Yes sir Charley replied he recognized The clipped clear tones of his old commanding officer.

Can you come to Richmond to see me tomorrow 10 o'clock sharp yes sir Charley replied his time in the army taught him no need to ask why he would know soon enough?

At 10 o'clock sharp Charley stood boots polished pressed shirt and trousers outside Lieutenant Colonel P J Midgley. He knocked on the door as the clock at the end of the passage ticked over to 10 o clock.

Come in come in sergeant Charley opened the door and walked in and stood in front of the chipped and scratched desk and saluted you are not in the service now Charley but I acknowledge your salute and he saluted Charley Please sit Thankyou sir Charley sat down after pulling up a chair.

Now sergeant parker you did three tours of Afghanistan six years ago and returned without a scratch yes sir said Charley very lucky No from what I gather from your comrades at the time you are an excellent soldier.

Sergeant I have to ask you this are you still up to the rigors of Afghanistan Charley was puzzled but his expression did not give it away Yes sir he replied.

Excellent said Lt Colonel PJ Midgley then I need you to do a very important and highly dangerous mission for your old regiment and your country How do you feel about that.

Excited Sir Charley replied.

Just as I anticipated said Lt Col Midgley Are you familiar with the north of Afghanistan in particular Herat its wild and still strongly Taliban There is a very high ranking Taliban leader there we are lead to believe he wants to defect but cannot leave the area on his own without suspicion.

This area has never been patrolled and is very pro-Taliban so we cannot send a service team in and we need a very experienced leader. In fact, we need you.

You will be sent in with a very trustworthy Afghany 3-man team and another ex-soldier Albert Donkin who served with you Kandahar.

Charley remembered Albert he was a tall raw boned Yorkshire man of few words but an excellent hard man a man to be relied on when the chips were down.

Col Midgley continued you will be dropped by a C14 at Kabul where will head for Herat.

I must make sure you are aware you and Albert will be a contractors and there will be no back up you will be on your own. One of the Afghanis knows the man Jahumbad ben Afarsie.

We need him back here alive he can be very valuable with his knowledge of Taliban hierarchy.

Ok Sir when do I leave.

Leaving here tomorrow can you make that 7 am.

Yes, sir I will be here replied Charley.

At 7 o'clock Charlies light blue Camry pulled up at the guard house a young corporal in the Green Howards insignia stepped out of the guard house ah morning Sargent he said with a grin back for more sir park over there please he indicated the adjacent parking across from the guard house they are waiting for you on the landing strip good luck Charley smiled back thanks corp.

He parked and walked over to the air field where a huge C15 stood with its rear door open and men were loading equipment Charley walked over to the tall man standing near Albert nice to see you how are they hanging?

Good Charley very good yours? the same Albert, the same.

Well here we go again Albert are you still up for it? never lost it Charley You? same Albert the same

Cl PHJ Midgley walked over with a couple of folders he gave one to each of them good luck chaps see you on your return and he shook hands with each of them.

On the tarmac the Afgharny was waiting He was a very dark Arab he stepped up to Charley and held his hand Useff barcoff he said to Charley.

Charley shook his hand it was dry and hard but he did not respond Charlie's grip which Charley thought was odd his dark eyes did not focus but flicked nervously back and forth Charley put it down to nervousness but had a slight doubt on the man's integrity and he thought he would warn Albert to keep tabs on Useff.

Useff Charley said I am told you know Ben Afarsie yes sir Useff replied he is my wife's cousin.

Oh, thought Charley the mans a relative but he made no comment.

Ok Charley said let's get this caravan on the move.

The massive transport plane now loaded with equipment guns' provisions and a battered Humvee REME engineers had extensively modified.

High tensile steel boiler plates 16 mm thick welded under the vehicle as protection from IED's.

The windows all fitted with bullet and shatterproof acrylic material and extra-large diesel tanks installed Harry Doud an engine specialist had lovingly gone over the engine special air filters developed to counter the conditions found in Afghanistan as well as the underbody, protection was added to the engine compartment. He also fitted self-inflating tires to counteract damage from bullets every detail checked and rechecked he was proud of his work.

As they sat on the canvas seats in the cavernous interior Charley opened the folders Col Midgley had given him with Albert looking over his shoulder.

In the folder was a photo of an Arab with a typical Taliban full beard and a beaded head cover.

He looked to be about 50-year-old with a lined and wrinkled skin where it could be seen mainly on his neck just above his left eye a scar ran up into his hair which pulled his eye slightly out of line it was an easily recognizable picture.

He handed the photo to Useff and watched carefully at his reaction it was slight but Charley noticed his mouth tightened.

Yes, he said that's Jehumbad how did he get the wound on his head Charley asked No idea said Useff last time I met him he didn't have a scar.

Again doubts came into Charlies thoughts the scar was obviously quite old so how long since he met him charley thought or was he lying He now had serious doubts about Useff.

The massive plane trundled up to the head of the giant runway and as the pilots opened the throttle the 4 engines rumble increased to a loud roar as it increased in speed until they were enough lift for it to rise and it cleared the ground.

The noise in the plane was so loud it was very difficult to talk so they sat in silence.

Useff with his secrets Charley with his doubts and Albert fast asleep Charley looked at Albert and smiled.

He had known Albert for a long time nothing ever ruffled him even in very tense and dangerous situations Albert was unflappable Charley could not wish for a better back up.

The flight to Kabul took 7 hours Charley joined Albert and slept for most of the flight while Useff alone with his thoughts sat in silence.

The door to the cock pit opened and the copilot stepped out Morning gents he addressed the passengers we are preparing to land at Kabul and he went back to join the pilot the landing was smooth in the heavily protected airport and when the plane stopped the huge cargo door at the rear opened up Quickly Albert drove the loaded Humvee out onto the runway.

The air was hot and humid the sun at 9 am was high and brassy shielding their eyes against the glare Charley and Useff joined Albert beside the Humvee.

A sergeant with the SAS approached them good morning he said and shook hands with Charley good to see you again Sarg he laughed O, Riley Charley laughed well done son last time we met you were a private nice to see you again.

I have been briefed on your mission Sarg.

Its Charley now son not Sargeant charley said No O, Riley said you will always be Sarg you have earned it you are a legend here I can tell you, you have no idea how often your story is told in the bar.

Anyway you will need these and he handed Charley 3 pairs of Dark goggles Your other two are waiting in the guard house they are good blokes both have family members killed by the ragheads so they are fiercely loyal.

Charley and Albert checked the equipment There was two SIG SAUER p320-M18 in under arm holsters.

5 AK- 103 updated auto assault rifles. 1 M82a1/M107Barrett long range sniper rifle and 500 round of ammunition for each.

Charley was happy with the selection his team was well armed.

Now he had to decide if he should allow his suspicions about Useff should prevent him being armed and decided for now not to rock the boat but be aware and at the first opportunity to inform Albert of his doubts about Useff.

The two Afghanis Achmed Feisal and George Oman Placed their two hands together and bowed slightly as they introduced to charley and Albert Have you been told of this operation Charley asked, they both confirmed they had Ok said Charley lets go.

Charley decided to make Useff their driver with Charley in the front seat he felt this was the best arrangement Albert and Achmed and George in the back.

They passed through the guarded front gates to the compound into Afghanistan a wild lawless country and hit the road to Herat The road to Panjab had been surfaced by the American troops.

From Panjab to Herat through Dowlat Yar and Chagcharin was a desert road hard but badly pot holed and sand blown.

Panjab was a typical Arab village town they stopped just outside for a drink and survival biscuits.

This is Taliban country and a lot of villages are sympathetic to their cause so be watchful George told them.

But there were no problems and they continued to Dowlat Yar This village was even more primitive and goats wandered in the main street people peered at them from the mud block houses the atmosphere was definitely hostile as they drove through the main street suddenly a shot and a bullet struck the windscreen without damage.

A bearded Arab in a dirty green outfit came out from behind a house and aimed a AK 47 at the Humvee Before he could fire his weapon Albert shot him through the from driver's side window he fell and another two came out and started firing Albert shot another and Charley shouted at Useff close the window and get us out of here.

Useff closed the window as a hail of bullet peppered the Humvee without any damage and he accelerated out of the village.

There were no further incidents until they approached Chagcharin This town appeared larger than the first two.

They stopped at a dilapidated petrol station on the outskirts of the town the two old Gilbarco pumps were old and battered Useff called the man inside the old building in Arabic Please fill up my vehicle the old man shuffled out and put the diesel hose into the tank and filled it up 120 Afghanis and 22 pulls he said to charley as he stepped up to pay the old man whispered in Arabic to Useff the Taliban are waiting in the town for you thank you uncle and he said to Charley give him a 100 Afghanis for his help The Taliban are waiting in the town he told Charley peeled off 200 Afghanis and gave then to the old man thank you he said the old man nodded and quickly disappeared inside.

There were 5 of the Taliban in the town they had placed a large truck across the road one was stood on the back of the truck with a shoulder mounted RPG.

Charley told Useff to stop the Humvee just short of 300m Before the barricade he knew the max range of an RPA was just short of 100 m jumping out taking the sniper rifle with him Charley rested it on the bonnet through the scope he picked up the man with the RPG centering on his chest he gently squeezed the trigger The 30-06 hit the man in the centre of his chest the RPG dropped to the truck bed and exploded killing all 4 men in the truck.

Charley and his team quickly drove the badly damaged truck out of the way and were soon on their way to Herat.

They arrived at the outskirts of Herat Ok Useff where will we find the man we want asked Charley.

The Taliban have their headquarters in an old bank building in town replied Useff.

In all probability the Taliban will be aware we are here or at least on our way.

Ok Useff said Charley this is where you come in you are a relative of Jehumbad and you are an Afgharny what do you suggest our next move should be.

I will go in alone and see if he will come out with me secretly ok no time like the present said Charley good luck we will be armed up and ready if you can bring this off it will save a great deal of trouble.

Useff set off and made his way to an old bank building in the town center two guards on the front do confronted him as he approached in Arabic he said greetings comrades I am Useff Jehumbad is my cousin I need to see him one of the guards using a sat nav phone spoke briefly and then said to Useff ok go in he is on the first floor room marked records Useff climbed the stairs thankful the guards had not searched him.

He knocked on the door marked records and an Arabic voice said yes it's me Useff. Useff said com in cousin Ussin entered the room Jehumbad was standing looking at a lap top on a desk.

Hey Useff, he said in surprise what are you doing here.

I came to see you about a family matter Useff walked round the desk a hugged Jehumbad at the same time in his right hand he held a long bladed double edged knife which he plunged into Jehumbad's stomach and pulled it up causing a fatal wound What the fuck was that exclaimed Jehumbad as he slumped into Useff arms.

Do you recall my son Ali he was 6 when he stood on one of your IEDs and was blown to bits that's for him and god blast you and all your like with his dying breath Jehumbad let out a scream?

From the next room two men ran into the records room Useff turned to meet them holding the bloody knife One of the men was holding a AK 47 and he raised it and emptied it into Useff on auto the gun pumped 30 bullets into him at point blank range.

At the end of the street the rapid gun shots were heard by Charley and the team Trouble said Charley lets go armed up they rushed toward the bank building the two guards had left the front and gone to investigate the commotion upstairs charley was first into the building followed closely by Alfred a man appeared at the top of the stairs with his gun on single shot Charley shot him hitting him in the chest he fell down the stairs.

Charley and Alfred ran up the stairs at the top the two guards rushed out of the records room Charley shot the first and Alfred the second down stairs there was a back stair as the first man came down Achmed shot him.

Upstairs a stream of bullets came through the records door just missing Alfred.

Charley kicked open the door and shot the last man as he desperately tried to fit a new clip into his weapon.

Is that the last Charley shouted clear here below shouted George all clear up here said Albert.

Charley went into the records room the man he knew from his scar to be Jehumbad lay behind the desk dead from a large stomach wound Useff was almost cut in half but his hand still held the knife

Well said Charley that explains a lot we have been shafted he came to kill him he wasn't interested in taking him back let get out of here said Alfred before the shit hits the fan.

there were two lap tops on the desk and a great deal of files Charley gathered them as they left and went down the stairs.

I think all this info could be as good as the man, said Charlie as they carefully exited the building.

Outside the building was quiet. Thy made it to the Humvee without incidents Albert took the driving seat.

Let's get out of here said Charley. They made good progress to within a couple of miles of Chagcharin.

As they came over the hill into the town They could see a great deal of activity with a massive road block on the outskirts.

Let's pull off the road until dark and assess our next move said Charley They pull off the road out of site of the town Charley climbed out and up the ladder attached to the back on the top was a large steel box Give me a hand Albert said Charley he opened the box and lifted up the hand held RPG and handed it down to Albert together with 3 rockets.

A little surprise package he explained laughing Two can play this game.

As dusk came albert and Charley reconnoitered the road block lying down below the skyline they could see again a large truck across the road. This time about 15 men walking around carrying.

AK 47s A large fire of burning tyres lit up the area Charley and Albert and the two others in the Humvee were about 750 m away.

When it's dark we have to get in range about 200 m Charley told Albert. Ok we will have to rely on Achmed and George to drive the Humvee I will use the RPG you must pick off as many as you can with an auto Charley told Albert Ok said Albert no sweat

Dark comes quickly in Afghanistan and within an hour it was jet black dark the burning tires casting a light area around the truck.

Charley and Albert silently and carefully picked their way down to the truck Charley had the tube and albert two rockets.

They could clearly see the truck by the fire light they approached without being discovered to about 200 m away Ok said Charley are you ready I am let give them a wakeup call while they at evening prayers he could see several men kneeling down with heads touching their prayer mats.

Charley knelt down and lined up the cab of the truck the largest target Albert placed the rocket in the tube and tapped Charley on the shoulder.

Charley gently stroked the trigger and with a whoosh the rocket sped towards the truck in a second the rocket hit the cab and exploded it blew the cab 5 meters to the left and lifted the bed and flung it to the right killing 4 of the men in close proximity to the blast.

Ok said charley let go while they are shell shocked.

They both ran forward the remaining men were actually disorientated walking about in shock they were quickly killed by Charley and Albert.

With the cease of gun fire the Humvee came trundling down the hill Charley and Albert climbed in quickly and they were off again

They travelled for about an hour before George said looking out of the back we have company a Ute with a machine gun mounted on the back was behind rapidly catching up.

Push the vehicle see if you can put a bit of distance from them.

The machine gun was a 50 Cal and a bullet hit the back door bulging it in and staring the window.

They topped a slight rise and for a few minute out of sight of the truck Achmed slowed and Charley jumped out carrying his rifle. He landed and crawled to a pile of rocks Hiding behind he chambered a round and waited as the truck topped the rise he picked out the man on the gun but as he pulled the trigger the truck bounced and the bullet flew wide.

The gunner immediately swung the gun round and shot in Charlies direction the heavy bullet causing rock splinters to shower Charley rapid fire came from the rear of the Humvee Albert had opened the door and blasted the front of the truck.

The gunner swung round to shoot at the Humvee a big mistake Charley quickly lined him up this time he hit the bearded man in the neck killing him instantly the gun swung loosely.

Another long burst from Albert killed the unprotected driver and his passenger the truck ran off the road and came to a halt.

Let's take the 50 Cal, Charley said, it's a very useful weapon they undid the gun and got it in the back of the Humvee with a magazine of 100 shells.

Back on the road again towards Dowlat Yar after about 2 hours They could see a slight glow in the sky ahead cutting the headlights they pulled the Humvee to the side of the road.

Using the night scope Charley scanned the source of the glow About 3 miles ahead was a large fire of burning tires and he could make out a lot of men some sitting others walking about. He counted at least 10.

He turned to Alfred. How much fuel have we left he asked Alfred checked the gauges we are on the reserve tanks he told Charlie so maybe another 20 miles.

WE need to find fuel there will be fuel available in the town so we have to neutralize the Taliban and find it.

We can't drive closer Charlie told his crew we will have to get down there on foot.

I will take the 50 Cal and find a spot where I can take out as many as I can but you will have to get close enough to take out the rest Albert you will come with me to spot and carry the ammo.

Achmed and George you will mop up the rest.

Taking the 50 Cal and a box of shells Charlie and Albert set off carefully in the dark they slowly made their way at about 750 yards they found a rock outcrop slightly to the left of the fire.

Albert looked through the night glasses and assessed the camp while Charlie set up the sniper's gun.

Dawn was starting to break, as the sky lightened Charlie adjusted the scope and looked down at the Taliban I cannot see any commanders he told Albert there are only foot soldiers and most seem to be quite relaxed they are probably expecting us to drive in.

Oh, oh Albert said up on the right hand side on top of the building is a rag head with a phone he is certainly a look out for warning the rabble round the fire.

Charlie raised the rifle and looked for him in the scope got him he said.

Any sign of our other team he asked Albert they are about 200 yards out coming in behind rocks on the right.

Ok Albert said Charlie we will give them as few minutes to get closer and I will take out the spotter.

All hell will break out when I shoot.

Ok replied Albert.

Charlie lined up the spotter putting the cross hairs on his chest.

Ok Charlie said Albert they are now about 100 yards out from the fire Hit him Charlie.

Charlie gently pulled back the bolt and slid a cigar shaped shell into the breech and closed the bolt.

Looking through the scope he breathed in and held it as he stroked the trigger.

Boom the man was sent backwards as the bullet hit him in the chest.

Charlie quickly swung onto the men before they realized what was had happened and shot another rag head as Achmed and George opened up on the rest running around uncoordinated they were quickly shot Charlie taking out another 2.

Ok Achmed go and fetch the Humvee Charlie told him.

Let's make sure there are no more Charlie and Albert Headed for the building where Charlie shot the spotter.

Carefully and cautiously they entered the building inside was a mess of wrappers and rubbish and stank of urine and fasces Going slowly up the stairs to the first floor they entered a room on the left here they found evidence of a communications set up a lap top and a short wave radio Charlie used his gun butt to smash the radio and take the lap top.

More useful info he told Albert.

As he bent to pick up the lap top he saw the yellow half brick of sematic with a red detonator sticking out.

For fucks sake Charlie roared get out Albert and they rushed to the stairs.

Up on the roof the seriously injured Taliban commander laughed as he sat against the parapet in his hand he held an old mobile phone Allahu Akbar he exclaimed (god is great) and he pressed the red button on the phone.

As they ran scrambling down the stairs the Semtex blew under the table bits of rubble showered down on Charlie and Albert

Albert stumbled and fell down the last flight Charlie got struck on his head but wasn't seriously injured Albert however when Charlie got to him was unconscious.

His left leg was bent underneath him and Charlie could see it was broken.

Achmed and George came into the building what happened Achmed exclaimed their com room was booby trapped Charlie told him we were on our way to check the spotter he must have survived and actuated the explosive.

Do you want me to check him out Achmed said?

Yes, go but be careful he was squarely hit but he might still be alive.

George can you find some timber we can use to carry Albert his leg is broken.

George returned with a piece of timber banister.

Using a field pack Charlie had straightened Alberts leg while he was still unconscious.

Then strapped the leg and administered a shot of morphine as Albert groaned and came too.

Fuck me Charley that was a close call.

In a small shed outside they found two 45 gal drums filled with diesel and a hand pump in one of the drums.

George said Charlie bring the Humvee as close as you can there is a 6 m hose on the hand pump fill up the tanks.

Meanwhile Achmed went carefully up the stairs to the roof Rifle at the ready he peered around the door across the other side he could see an Arab sitting with his back to the wall slumped to one side.

A small black phone had slipped from his hand he was dead.

They loaded Albert on his makeshift stretcher into the Humvee and set off for their final town of Panjab.

They passed through without any problems About half a mile out of town at a slight bend in the road the rear wheel hit an IED which blew off the complete wheel and suspension.

Fortunately no one was hurt due to the vehicles protection But now they were seriously in trouble they were still 100miles from Kabul.

Go back into the village see if you can find a vehicle Charlie said to Achmed and he gave him, a 1000 US dollars if necessary buy one.

In a couple of hours Achmed returned driving an old battered Toyota land cruiser with a cracked windscreen and smashed back windows.

I got it for $ 500 he told Charlie handing him back $400 Charlie counted the money and looked at Achmed.

Achmed smiled and showed him the front seat of the Toyota a ham and fruit and several piles of flat bread and as well a pack of bottles of water Good man Charlie said and slapped him on the shoulder.

The Set fire to the Humvee and loaded the Toyota Giving Albert another shot of morphine.

The journey back to Kabul was uneventful and they arrived at the compound in 3 hours.

Handing over all the information and lap tops.

The de briefing took 4 hours.

Charles Parker, Col Midgley addressed Charley you have done yourself proud and given us a treasure trove of information thank you.

Charley stood beside the hospital bed and looked down at Albert.

Well Albert he said Doc says you will be good as new in a few months.

I have negotiated a handsome Pay out for you and the others for your efforts.

Thanks Charlie Albert told him You are the best I have ever served with.

If you need me again Charley for an adventure, please contact me I enjoyed the adrenalin. Ok keep well Albert and he walked out of the ward.

Charlie arrived home 2 days later and immediately his phone rang It was Jimmy Hi charley he said am I glad you are back.

Why what's the problem? Jimmy said Charley.

The police came and discovered the gun room fuck said Charley how did that happen I don't know they made a more thorough search and discovered it but don't worry I had already removed all the guns and other stuff.

I will come over straight away Jimmy said Charley. Ok replied Jimmy.

They were sat in the old elm chairs in the kitchen with a whiskey each.

Ok Jimmy what happened said Charley.

My sister works in the Harrogate police station she rang me from the toilets to say there was going to be a raid on the farm.

So I moved all the guns and ammo straight away I had a premonition they may find the room my sister said they were very excited at the station.

So where are the guns now Jimmy? Charley asked. In the barn under a plastic sheet with a ton of mangles over them in a cart Charley laughed.

I was very careful they are all ok but I only just finished when they arrived 10 of them This time they were determined to find something.

At first I thought we would be OK they were there about two hours and I thought they were ready to give up when a young keen copper shouted over here he had discovered the hatch.

They were ecstatic and all rushed into the barn laughing all that changed when they went down the room was empty.

All stood around with serious faces two even leaning on the cart

They took me in to the station and grilled me I told them my dad made the room to store his home made wine they didn't believe me but there was nothing they could do so after a couple of hours they let me go.

But said they wanted to talk to you.

I told them you were away on army business and I would tell you when I saw you.

Ok great thanks Jimmy.

No probs Charley we will have to find another hiding place.

As expected Charley was sat outside his new caravan drinking a coffee when his phone rang.

Mr. Parker Yes said Charley Good morning sir this is DC Oldfield here good morning said Charley.

Can you pop into the station today please OK inspector what is the problem?

I will explain when you come in.

Charley sat in the interview room and patiently waited DC Oldfield and a woman entered.

Sorry for the wait Mr. Parker Dc Oldfield said I am going to record this meeting he said and turned on the recording machine.

Ok the date is the 12 of July 2007 present DC Oldfield, constable Haywood and he nodded at Charley.

On the 11 of July this year we conducted a search on long Bank farm owned by one of your colleagues Mr. James Kendrick are you aware of what we found.

No said Charley I am not I have been in Afghanistan on army business Yes I am aware I contacted Col Midgley who sang your praises with gusto.

Charley said Nothing in response.

So why am I here he asked.

We found a hidden room at the said farm which Mr. Kendrick said his father built to store his homemade wine.

Well he did once tell me his dad made wine Charley replied. But I still don't understand what you want from me.

We believe the room was only built recently.

Well said Charley again what is that to do with me were you aware of this room Mr. Parker.

No, said Charley.

DC Oldfield was now clearly exasperated Are you absolutely sure you know nothing about this room he almost shouted.

Now Charley stood up I have told you I know nothing about any room at Jimmies farm now if there is nothing else I have better things to do than answer your stupid questions You have done your level best recently to incriminate me in different crimes for which you have no evidence and I am now going I cannot help you any further.

Charley walked out of the police station chuckling to himself.

Good old Jimmy he thought.

DC Oldfield watched him walk across the car park through the window and shook his head.

The forensic team had found traces of gun oil in the room which had convinced DC Oldfield there.

was more to this room than wine storage but the lack of any proof he had to give up on his pursuit of Charley Parker.

For the time being!

The British Army Paid Albert Donkin $10000 for his part in the trip to Afghanistan trip.

Charley received $15000 Achmed and George unfortunately as serving soldiers received only a commendation for their efforts.

For a few months Charley and Jimmy discussed a new gun storage they removed the guns and ammunition from under the mangles to behind some straw bales in the barn not really a permanent hiding place but it would have to do until they could work out a new place.

A few weeks later Charley was sitting outside his new caravan on a camping chair with a cup of tea.

An old Toyota pickup pulled up outside and a large recognizable man climbed out it was Daz.

Charley put down his cup of tea and rose to meet him.

Daz approached and held out both arms with his palms out in front Mr. Parker he said You have more than proved yourself I would just like to talk to you please if you can spare me a moment.

Ok said Charley see no threat at all he beckoned him to a seat and he sat down. Ok charley said go ahead.

Daz to a deep breath about a couple of years ago Royston smith my old boss sent me to Manchester to a small old shop just out of town what connection he had with the shop I never found out but the old lady running it was having trouble with the Indian mafia in Manchester I sorted out the Indians and left the old lady Mrs. Western my card.

She phoned me yesterday and told me the Indians have returned no doubt they have heard that the Eland road organization has been disbanded.

Charley looked at him I know I know Daz said but I am on parole and the police monitor my movements and I know what you think of me but Mrs. Western does not deserve this intimidation again and I cannot think of anybody more capable of helping than you.

Charley thought for a moment then turned and looked at Daz I am surprised he said thought fully but perhaps there is some small good in you.

Give me the address and I will sort it out.

Daz rose from his chair and handed Charley a note with the address. Thank you he said and held out his hand Charley stared into his face then smiled and shook his hand once again Daz felt the power behind the smaller man.

The next day Charley caught the train to Manchester and the Uber driver drove him to the address on the piece of paper Daz had given him.

As he opened the door the little bell pinged and the elderly lady came into the shop from behind the curtain. Yes, sir can I help you she said to Charley.

No he said I am here to help you the big man you rang in Leeds cannot come so he asked me my name is Charley can we go somewhere to talk.

Of course, she said and walked past Charley to the door and turned the open sign to closed Charley followed her to the rear to the tiny lounge behind the curtain please sit she said would you like a cup of tea yes please said Charley milk and two sugars.

They sat on two chairs facing each other at the small dining table Charley could see she was nervous her wrinkled hands were shaking Charley reached over and took her hands she looked at him and tears appeared and ran down her cheeks.

Come on Charley said we can sort this out easily but you have to be honest with me please this is not straight forward there are not nice people involved how did the man Daz get involved.

Mrs. Western drew a deep breath and brushed away her tears.

The shop is owned by a man called Mr. Tindal he used to come every month and check the takings and take the money he hasn't been here for the last 6 months Now he rings me up and I tell him how much the takings are and he gave me a bank account and I deposit the money into it.

When Mr. Daz came he hit the Indian who was taking money from the till and I had no more trouble until this week when they the Indians came back and took money again and said they would be back every week. They are due back tonight I am so scared.

Ok said Charley Mr. Tindal is in jail for corruption he was the assistant chief constable of Yorkshire.

He will not be around for another 10 years The Man Daz was part of a Leeds crime syndicate similar to the Indians you are having trouble with which was involved with Assistant chief constable Tindal.

The boss of that gang is also in jail.

Now I will sort the Indians out you must now stop putting the money in Tindals bank account you keep it for yourself by the time Tindal gets out of jail you must retire close the shop and can you leave Manchester.

Yes, my daughter lives in Cornwall she keeps asking me to go and live with her there.

Ok good now when Tindal rings you again tell him Charley parker has taken over the shop and there will be no more money can you do that I think you will find he will not be a problem I am the main reason he is in jail.

Suddenly Mrs. Western picked up yes I can she said.

What time do the Indians come said Charley in about 30 mins Ok let have another cuppa.

Mrs. Western was behind the counter Charley stood at the side when they arrived there were three the first two small and stringy the last was huge a steroid giant he turned to Charley and said fuck off home grandad.

Charley grinned and closed and locked the door carefully turning the open sign to closed this surprised the giant Indian.

Hay Hamad we have a joker here he said and he grinned two of his canine teeth had been ground to sharp points the two other Indians turned and laughed he walked towards Charley with a menacing grin As he approached Charley casually picked up a tin of beans oh is that for your dinner granddad The Indian laughingly said No its for you said Charley What the idiot did not see that in this left hand Charley held a crow bar he had brought in his back pack like a striking snake Charley brought it down on the giants muscular fore arm snapping the bone and dislocating his elbow the man roared in pain and hugged his injured arm Stepping in close he hit the man's jaw with the tin of beans breaking it in two places as the man bent forward to try and ease the pain charley brought up his knee into his face his nose split and as he slumped on the floor the blood spurted He was the muscle the other two just looked at his body in shock Now get this fool out of here and if you come back be prepared for wheelchairs and get an ambulance for this goon.

Also tell your boss at the blue lantern to expect me.

The Indians never came near the shop again and after Charlies visit to the Blue lantern it was made clear of the consequences if they attempted too.

Harry Tindal phoned Mrs. Western a week later and asked her about the deposit amounts Mrs. Western now pumped up after Charlies visit told him what Charlie had told her. For a few seconds there was a silence on the phone and she heard a shout from another person. Hey hurry up wanker then Harry said oh fuck and the line went dead she never heard from him again.

Things were not going well for harry in Wakefield Police usually had to be housed in isolation for their safety It had been a bad 18 months for Harry Even in isolation prisoners found ways to get to him Feces in his food A prison guard was paid to stick a pencil in his eye and trip him up on his way to the bathroom which also lost him his front teeth as the guard stamped on the back of his head as he lay on the floor he had also lost a lot of weight.

Mrs. Western stayed at the shop for the next 8 years and with the money she saved she packed her bags on close of business a Friday night and caught the train to Truro her daughter picked her up and she left to retire with her daughter at Coverack.

Before she left on Friday evening She crafted a letter to the Chief Constable and posted it care of DCI George Leftbridge Manchester central police station.

The letter read;

Dear Sir,

The shop at 15 Wallace Terrace and High Street, Manchester Is I believe owned by ex-Assistant Chief Constable Harry Tindal Who I understand was found guilty of corruption and jailed for 10 years I believe that this property was acquired by corrupt means.

Yours Faithfully,

A concerned citizen.

Mrs. Western left no footprint and was never traced she lived in retirement in the small Cornish village she died at 95.

DCI Leftbridge forwarded the letter to the Chief constable who instructed the DCI to investigate the claims in the letter. Searching the property records George found the hidden details of the ownership of the shop.

Reading the trial transcript of Harry Tindal, He was not surprised it had not been listed in his assets.

An application was made in the Manchester central court to a acquire the property and contents the magistrate examined the details of the application and agreed to the proposal. He signed the order.

The shop and contents were sold and the proceeds went into council revenue.

After Charley returned from Manchester, his life returned to normal relaxing in his garden and sitting in Jimmy's kitchen looking at the fire through the bottom of their whisky glasses.

I oiled all the guns today Charley said Jimmy mm said Charley we will have to work out a more permanent hiding place.

Actually I do not think the police will come again but it's too much of a risk to use the underground room again just in case. They are convinced that I was responsible for doing all the Bikies even though they have been unable to prove it they won't give up so let's not take any chances with the guns, It would be the proof they need to charge me.

Well said jimmy they are ok for now I have put more bales in the barn.

And with that Jimmy threw another pear log on the fire and they settled back in the old elm high backed chairs and sipped the single malt.

About 3 months after Charley returned from Afghanistan He woke up with a start at first he could not really identify the noise Quickly pulling on his pants and an old cardigan he opened his caravan door. The flood light illuminated his garden 3 teenager's stood on his lawn they appeared to be 14 or 15 years old they were all wearing hoodies on had a baseball bat the other two one had a carving knife the other a machete.

The one with the machete stepped towards Charley.

Give us your fucking keys grandad he said Charley laughed piss off boys before you get in any deeper he said.

The boy advanced and as he approached he raised the machete don't be silly old man all we want is your keys do yourself a favor and save yourself from harm.

Again Charley laughed and the kid walked forward and raised the machete ok I warned you the kid said and he struck at Charlies shoulder Charley blocked his arm with his left hand and at the same time trapped his arm with his right and locked it with his left arm he applied pressure and with an audible crack the kids skinny arm bone broke and the machete fell from his nerveless hand the kid screamed Charley released him and he fell holding his broken arm the largest of the other two rushed forward holding the knife nervously in front of him.

As he lunged at Charley, Charley stepped to one side and with his fist clenched using his arm like a club Charley swung and hit him breaking his jaw the kid fell like a log his mouth hanging open the other kid dropped the knife and fled down the street.

Charley phoned police and emergency services.

George Bentley, Arther Tiplady and John smith were all well known to police.

George Bentley was on parole being accused of car theft and armed robbery.

Arther Tiplady also on parole for bag snatching and demanding money with menaces.

John Smith Car theft but not convicted as he was a passenger in a stolen car driven by George Bentley.

In the hospital George Bentley had his broken arm reset but the break was compound and there was severe nerve damage the surgeon doubted he would fully recover the use of his right hand

Arther Tiplady needed his jaw to be wired shut, it was broken in two places, and he had bitten his tongue and lost two front teeth snapped off at the gum the whole of his right hand side of his face was a mass of purple bruises.

John Smith was arrested at his home in the Railway Street Caravan site his parents quite used to the police arriving at their caravan Billy smith answered the door to the police he was unsteady on his feet and held on to the door frame to stop him falling over in his other hand a bottle of half-drunk beer.

What the fuck do you lot want know he slurred.

PC Alice Brownlow looked at his bloodshot eyes. Is your son here? She asked. No he said he is with his grandmother no 56 now fuck off he said and slammed the door.

Granny Smith was a Romany gypsy the head of the Smith clan Her Sister Piri Tollington was the matriarch of the Tollington empire. PC Brownlow knocked apprehensively on no 56 caravan, pleased she had 2 large male constables with her.

She had had many dealings with granny Smith in the past she was a formidable woman. Apart from Billy she had another five children all living in the caravan compound living on the very edge of the law but cunning enough to avoid prosecution.

Granny Smith answered PC Brownlow's knock. She was indeed an imposing woman standing six foot two inches her head shaved smooth as an egg she looked down at PC Brownlow.

I smell pork she drawled, John get your fucking self out here now she shouted The pigs are here for your young wanker what the fuck have ya done this time.

He is implicated in a house invasion and armed robber PC Brownlow explained.

Implicated.

Granny Smith exclaimed Oh he was there PC Brownlow started to explain, what Granny Smith shouted with those other two counts she shouted she turned and slapped John on the back of his head.

How many times have I told you to keep away from them she shouted.

Well he wasn't involved in the actual violence PC Brownlow explained but he threatened the caravan owner with a baseball bat.

And said Granny Smith Well the caravan owner put the other two in hospital with very serious injuries and Johnny here ran off.

Who was this hero asked Granny Smith A man it does not pay to tangle with Replied PC Brownlow.

Ok Granny Smith said take the little fucker and she pushed John out.

DI Oldfield sat in the interview room opposite George Bentley The date is 11-dec 2022 Present DI Oldfield and PC Brownlow, Anne Claymore from child services and Your name for the tape please Michael Mouse said George and giggled George Bentley said D I Oldfield. Please don't be stupid son said The DI you are in trouble and I understand you will lose the use of your right hand.

Yes, and what are you going to do too the old man who did this We only asked him if he needed help with his garden.

At 3-30 in the morning? and carrying a machete Well we forgot the time and I was not carrying a machete it was my phone.

Oh said the DI So how come we found a machete at the scene with your fingerprints on it.

You have faked it to implicate me in a crime.

Oh is that so said the Di Your comrade in arms John Smith has agreed to testify the truth.

That fucking Gypo he cannot tell the truth if his life depended on it George exclaimed.

Well that went well The DI said to PC Brownlow as they walked away from the interview I cannot believe he is only 16 his wrap sheet is more than six pages.

In the detention centre John Smith was in the shower a 18 year old offender appeared at the shower cubicle and moved the shower curtain to one side John was facing the shower head with his back to the curtain using a sharpened tooth brush he stabbed John in his kidneys twice John collapsed onto the shower floor blood pumping out of the wounds the 18 year old turned and walked to a grate picking up the grate he dropped the tooth brush into the open drain first wiping his finger prints off on his pants and walked out of the shower that cost George two small pink tablets.

Georg Bentley left home at 14 he was unable to accept either his parents discipline or the teachers at his school he found the restrictions pointless so for the next two years he had lived in the streets he actually had a high IQ he was clever even with his self-opinionated view of himself the police arrested him numerous times and he had appeared in the juvenile courts numerous times He had been placed in juvenile detention, parole and good behavior bond But during this time he had learned his age prevented the courts in giving him more onerous punishment so he progressed to more serious crimes.

Until he ran into Charley parker. He had had no trouble in intimidating old ladies and more weaker people he was a big lad for his age. The hospital had taken off his plaster cast but sadly his hand did not function at all. He even thought of having it removed and hook fitted but thought perhaps in the future he could get it fixed a forlorn hope however the damage was permanent.

With the police past dealings with Charley they persuaded the public prosecutor to prosecute Charley for using excessive force during his home invasion.

So once again Charley was arrested and charged and released on his own recognizances and once again he phoned QC Harvey Waterman in Cross Gates, Leeds.

Hello Charley you in trouble again said Harvey Yes Sir replied Charley can you find time see me.

Of course let me give you a time.

Ok said Harvey I am free tomorrow at 10 is that convenient I will be there replied Charley.

When Harvey had read Charlies statement he looked up. At charley Well it looks like to me as a slam dunk Charley I cannot see the sense in charging you after the last time.

Well said Charley neither can I as the last pressure to charge me came from the commissioner now in prison for corruption but i suppose the police in general have long memories and don't like losing.

Ok Charley I will represent you let their prosecutor know.

The case for George Bentley and Arthur Tiplady was set for the 3 Feb.

The two remaining boys were sentenced to 4 years juvenile detention for George as he was classed as the ringleader and 2 years for Arthur. Mr. Bentley the magistrate addressed George the next time you come before the court should you not improve yourself you will be an adult and the court will not be so lenient.

George gave the magistrate the Vee sign as he was escorted out of the court to start his sentence.

Charlies case was two days later.

The prosecuting council was first to outline the case, this case is about accused man a very experienced soldier who was the victim of an assault in the morning of 9th of Dec last year where 3 young boys attempted to steal the accused's vehicle during this attempted robbery two of these young boys received at the hands of this experienced ex-soldier terrific injuries far exceeding what could be considered reasonable force. We will show the court the nature of these injuries one of which will mean the child has lost the use of his arm for the rest of his life.

Harvey stood to give the defense's case.

The prosecution has given you an eloquent explanation of their reason for prosecuting my client but the truth of this matter is far different from their simplistic statement.

The three young thugs which the prosecution refers to as children two of them were violent young criminals previously convicted among many other crimes of malicious wounding, intimidation and robberies with menaces and in fact already on bail for some of these crimes.

The one losing the use of his right arm attacked my client with a machete with the obvious intent of causing massive injuries when my client refused to give him his vehicle keys when my client disarmed him one of the others rushed at him with a knife in an attempt to stab him.

These three had learned that violence got them what they wanted and they used this to intimidate with impunity elderly people and women until they tried to intimidate and rob what they thought was a middle aged man, easy prey.

If you poke a wasps nest you must expect to get stung.

The prosecution offered no witnesses as they considered the two boys unreliable but Harvey had no qualms calling them.

George Bentley was the first called up by Harvey he was escorted into the witness box and sworn in Can you please tell the court what you were doing on the morning of the 9th of Dec where you committed a crime for which you have been convicted and sentenced to 4 years' detention is that correct.

George looked at Harvey then at Charley no it bloody well is not said George I have been fitted up for this using this gangster like term thinking it made him sound good Oh What are you saying Mr. Bentley you were not there No we were there replied George but not to harm the old fool we just needed to borrow a phone to ring for a lift what armed with a machete and a knife and a baseball bat No the police placed them at the house Oh is that right Mr. Bentley how do you think the machete had your finger prints on it.

The police put them there they had my prints from a previous time George retorted Oh and how did Mr. Tiplady and Mr. Smith's prints got on the knife and baseball bat found at the scene do you think.

That's now to do with me he shouted He held up his damaged arm look what the bastard did to me he shouted.

We have a statement from Mr. Smith which disagrees with your testimony here today.

Harvey handed a paper to the clerk who took it to the magistrate.

Well it's a fucking lie said George the magistrate said to him Mr. Smith moderate your language please.

Fuck off replied George.

Please remove Mr. Bentley from the court he said to the court security guards I will not have this type of behavior in this court. I will hold you in contempt and deal with you later.

Will the defense and prosecutor Please approach the bench he said.

This is a farce I will not have this kind of behavior I am going to dismiss this case and award costs to Mr. Parker step back.

So Once again Charley survived the police prosecution and came out with his record clean a great deal of annoyance to DI Oldfield.

I cannot believe the luck of this man he told PC Brownlow he seems to be able to do the most horrendous crimes and walk away without a scratch. I have read his file said the PC he certainly seems to have an angel on his shoulder. More like the devil the DI grumbled but I have a feeling we will cross paths again.

Meanwhile George Bentley sat on his bed in his lovely little room at the juvenile detention center and s.

Charley was shopping in Wetherby, as he came out of Tesco in the markets carrying a plastic Tesco bag he was aware he was being watched.

The woman was old and frail which intrigued Charley he saw her when he entered Tesco and she was still there when he left.

Charley walked across the road and walked down main street turning into market square in the bank windows he saw the woman had followed him he turned into a side street and then quickly into a ginnal which took him behind me.

John is in trouble she explained he is my only relative left I brought him up from a tiny baby until he joined the army.

Again why are you here not him Charley asked puzzled.

He is to ashamed she explained.

Ashamed charley exclaimed you had better explain.

When john left the army he had a bad time adjusting to life outside the army he sank down into a bad place. Started drinking and even worse taking drugs he was severely depressed there was nothing I could do to get him out of this state.

Then a week ago he came to my house, he had been badly beaten he had been to the hospital casualty and they patched him up but he was very badly shaken.

I finally got him to explain. He had foolishly agreed to deliver a package to an address in Leeds the package was in a black holdall he did not ask what it was but I think he suspected it was drugs in fact it was cocaine worth a million pounds.

He was in very poor health by this time from depression, drugs and alcohol.

The address was in one of the post war block of flats in Leeds. He got off the bus outside the flats as he walked in several teenagers attacked him with bricks and took the holdall. When he came too they and the holdall were gone. After the hospital discharged him he came to my house where he has hidden since then. He doesn't think the dealers who gave him the drugs know where I live but he is very concerned they may find out.

I know John looks up to you and on his leave with me he often talked about you but I know now he is to ashamed to ask you for help so I decided to find you. I love john he is all I have left and I fear that something dreadful is going to happen if these people come looking for him.

She started crying again come on cheer up Charley stood up and put his arm around the old lady I will come home with you see what we can do.

Where do you live, he asked in Garforth she said. How did you get here? Charley asked. On the bus she told him.

Ok charley said come on my car is in the car park lets go and see John.

Annie lived in a small council flat on Leeds road. When they arrived Charley parked the car in the car park and they walked round the block to her front door.

The door was open and had been forced the jamb was splintered.

Stay hear Charley told her he went inside the flat was empty cupboards and draws ripped open and contents scattered all over the floor.

On the kitchen table was a note written on a piece of paper

"If yoose want 2 C this bozo again we need the bag back 336-0489.

If we have 2 cum back yoose will be sorry.

It took Charley and Annie 3 hours to put everything back and tidy up. What are we going to do now? Annie said her voice quavering.

I am going to ring these people said Charley let's find out who we are dealing with first.

In the old Embassy cinema Elland road crime organizations office, a mobile phone hooted a black man with dreadlocks picked up the phone yes he drawled "what can this cat do for ya".

I have your bag Charley answered. Where is John if he is dead your bag goes into the river.

We have him here he's not good but he is alive Now if you don't bring the back now I will kill him do you hear me bozo.

Give me the address I will be there said Charley.

Where asked Charley the Old Embassy cinema Elland road the black man said Get a move on Bozo.

On his way Charley stopped at two places First the army and navy stores on boar lane where he purchased a black holdall and secondly a building site in Elland road where in as rubbish skip he got 8 bricks which he wrapped in paper he also found in the skip and placed them in the bag.

Carrying the bag, he entered the cinema a huge heavily tattooed man stood in the entrance, legs apart arms folded. Gimmi the bag grandad he grunted come and get it Charley replied. The man stepped slowly forward He approached Charley and stopped a few feet away a mistake he was too confident in his size and his abilities to intimidate drop the bag bozo he grunted Charley dropped the heavy back and as it fell the man's eyes watched it another mistake He missed the heavy redwing boot as it smacked into his balls he grunted and bent forward in extreme pain where the redwing boot again contacted his jaw breaking it in two places He fell in a crumpled heap on the tiled floor blood leaking from his shattered jaw.

Another black man with dreadlocks stepped out of an office a few feet away what have you done to Pony he exclaimed as he stared at the man on the floor He bent and pulled a long double edged knife from a holder strapped to his leg. He pointed the knife at Charley. Ok let's have it he before I cut ya.

Charley threw the bag on the floor at his feet he bent and unzipped it opening the paper he saw the bricks, just before Charley grabbed the arm holding the knife What the fuck he exclaimed it was too late Charley grabbed his wrist with his left hand placing his right arm behind the man's elbow and grabbing his left arm with his right hand as he applied pressure the tendons in the man's elbow gave way and he screamed the knife dropped from nerveless fingers.

Where is he Charley asked and he squeezed harder the man screamed again in the office he squeaked and nodded to the office he had just come out of.

Charley released the arm and pushed him through the door.

John was slumped in a chair his face was a mess another black man stood over him holding a small silver pistol Charley was holding the knife dropped by the man with dreadlocks with a flick of his wrist he threw the knife the knife flew and hit the man in the neck.

With blood pulsing from the wound he collapsed Charley picked up the pistol.

The man with the dreadlocks whose name was Moses had never experienced more pain than he was now with his badly dislocated elbow He hugged it to his chest in an attempt to ease the stabbing pain he got every time it moved.

Charley used the office phone and ordered a taxi to take John back to Annie's flat.

Moses passed out when he came too he was seated in a chair.

Charley was sitting on the desk he had removed the knife and wiped his finger print off it wrapping Moses limp hand onto the handle.

He looked a Charley with pain filled bloodshot eyes Who the fuck is you he asked Just a friend of the man you kidnapped Moses managed a weak smile oh yes like I believe you.

I don't care what you think Charley told him what I want to know now is who owns those drugs I can't see you able to purchase a million pounds worth of drugs Oh fuck you don't realize what a dangerous position we are all in now The drugs belong to the Sinolian cartel one of the largest drug cartels in Mexico If and when they find out and they will they will send men here to find out what has happened to their money.

Well Moses I suggest that when they do you are honest with them and dream up whatever story your fertile mind can concoct. They do not worry me at all and if they come for me they may not find it as easy as they think.

When Royston Smith was charged and convicted his criminal organization was disbanded his money confiscated and his assets sold. (see Charley Parker adventure no 1) One of his assets was the old now renovated Embassy cinema which Moses picked up   at a public auction it was financed by Panzarala Sinolia Which the cartel used as its UK centre of operations in Europe. Putting Moses in charge and up to now it had been a good investment it was growing rapidly.

Now with the loss of a million pounds in drug capital it was in trouble real trouble and Moses as the head was also in trouble and he knew it.

Sitting in the office with his badly damaged shoulder in plaster he desperately sought a way out.

His dead man Tommo had gone to Teumeo's Jamaican funeral parlor to be cremated pony had his jaw wired and on light duties.

What a mess all from one old grandad he had been unable to get any information on the man at all what was he going to tell the cartel which he knew was coming.

It came a week later in the form of three hard looking grim faced men the leader Panzarelas brother Manola.

These men were animals when Moses tried unsuccessfully tried explain the loss of the drugs Manola grabbed his damaged arm and pulled him out of the chair he was sitting in the plaster cast broke and Moses screamed as Manola twisted it pulling apart the healing tendons. Moses again fainted with the extreme pain.

When he came too he was in a chair his legs taped together his arms taped behind his back. Manola stood over him where do I find this old man he roared Moses stammered I don't know but the man who he came to find lives with his grandma at flat 27- 89 Leeds road Garforth his name is John Now we are getting somewhere Manola said Holding his chin and the back of his head he jerked his head first to the left then right then back breaking his neck.

Manola pulled up in the rented Mercedes outside the housing complex he walked around looking for no 27 when he found it he knocked on the door Annie answered the door.

She saw Manola and tried to shut the door he pushed her and walked in Where is John he asked I don't know she said he didn't come here when he got out of hospital.

Manola grabbed her with his hands over her ears he broke her neck He put her body on the settee looking round he found her phone Looking at the numbers he started with the latest at the third number a man said Annie is everything all right how is John.

If you want to see granny alive you had better come to her flat Manola grunted The phone cut out.

Charley left immediately and arrived in Garforth 45 minutes later Parking his battered Toyota in the nearby pub car park he walked quickly to the units crossing the courtyard he went to the rear of 27.

Keeping low he peered through the kitchen window through the kitchen he could see into the lounge and Annie's legs on the settee but one slipper had fallen off it was clear to Charley she was either dead or unconscious.

Slipping a credit card under the lock tongue he opened the door and slipped into the small kitchen carefully he crept to the lounge door a large man was sat in a chair looking out of the lounge windows using his silenced star 9 mm he shot the man in the right knee fucking hell the man roared and tried to stand his leg giving way he fell back in the chair Charley stood in front of him looking down his leg was badly damaged Charley shot him in the left knee the man moaned do you know who I am he stuttered I don't care replied Charley you just killed an old lady I liked now who are you apart from a cripple I am the brother of Panzanala Sinolia Who is that a pizza maker said Charley.

It's the largest drug cartel in Mexico said Manola.

Well said Charley its now short of a member.

Charley picked up Annie's phone and gently closed her eyes He threw the phone into Manola's lap.

First he said where are the rest of you are not here alone.

Manola was now worried he realized this was no ordinary middle-aged man they are in the railway hotel in Leeds.

Well you can ring the pizza man and tell him you have run into trouble and you are finished here.

He won't accept that Manola said you have no idea who you are dealing with.

Neither do you Charley replied Now ring him Manola phoned his brother and spoke in Spanish. He closed the phone and looked at Charley I warned you he is coming himself.

I hope he brings a lot with him Charley laughed Where does he live asked Charley in Campeche on the gulf anybody in the area will tell you where his house is.

Great said Charley and he shot Manola between the eyes.

Before he left Charley picked up the phone and rang the last number on the dial

When the call was answered Charley said is that the pizza man who is that a heavily accented voice replied If you want your brother he is at flat 27 -87 Leeds road Garforth near Leeds be quick he is starting to smell.

Charley closed the phone and tossed it into Mamola's lap He left the flat drawing the curtains and locking the doors.

Charley sat in Jimmies kitchen and swirled the Laphroaig around in the jam jar well Jim boy it looks like we have got another military op on our hands Ok said Jimmy what have you got into now Charley.

Charley related what had transpired.

What I have to decide now Jim is how I deal with this do I wait for them to come over here or pre-empt that and go to Mexico.

Jimmy thought for a while well he finally said what are you thinking if you go over there bust up his empire while he is occupied here well you certainly have the experience operating overseas Charley Jim said.

Yes, Charley mused staring into his jam jar I will contact the Donk see if he is up for a bit of excitement Albert Donkin the phlegmatic Yorkshire man who was with Charley on his recent Afghanistan foray If his leg ok now.

Eh up Albert Charley said using Alberts Yorkshire dialect Are you up to scratch I have an adventure if you are up for a bit of excitement Eh up Charley "is the pope catholic" was his reply.

What's the mission this time.

This is a personal matter replied Charley so it's entirely up to you, no cover, no money, no back up Charley if it's for you, you know you can count on me one hundred percent.

Give me the details. Ok Albert meet me in the Bay horse in Wetherby tomorrow at 12 is that ok. Sure Charley I will be there.

Charley and Albert sat in the snug bar at the Bay horse.

Ok Charley give me the story Albert said.

Charley took a slug of his John Smiths Bitter and told Albert the story When he had finished Albert stared out of the snug windows onto the market square I remember John Albert finally said, he was a good kid it's a shame he has ended up in this state how is he going.

The death of his grandma has shocked him out of his poor state I think he will be ok I have got him into a private clinic up in Scotland out of the way as I think the cartel will be looking for him.

So Albert Charley said what do you think.

Albert thought for a while then said I think we go and hit them at home while they are over here I agree said Charley I will book flights today for Mexico.

We will fly to Mexico City and hire a car it's about a 5 drive to Campeche.

We won't have military equipment we will have to improvise Albert laughed not the first time Charley nor the last added Charley.

The British Airways 777300ER landed in the international airport.

Albert and Charley picked up their bags from the luggage elevator.

And headed to the hire car booth The lady thankfully spoke English so in a short time they picked up the Toyota in the car park using a map in the car the set off for Campeche.

At the same time The Dassault falcon 7x landed at Leeds and Bradford airport and Panzanala and three heavies embarked The three men who arrived with Mamola were parked outside in a black range rover Panzanala climbed into the rear seat and the other three piled in Take me to this address he said to the driver and he gave him the address on a piece of paper written on it Flat 27 - 87 Leeds Rd, Garforth.

Keep a look out for a camping store We will need a sleeping bag. Panzanala told his men.

They stopped at Camping Inc. in Leeds and one of the men bought a sleeping bag.

The flat was still locked looking around to see it was deserted.

Kick it open Panzanala told his men and the went in The smell told then what had happened luckily the flies had not got to the bodies they put Manola in the sleeping bag and left.

The cartel had acquired a rundown abattoir off Rooley lane at a industrial complex in Bradford which they now operated as a pork abattoir it had an old incinerator to dispose of unwanted animal waste at two AM on Sunday Panzanala and his three men entered the building carrying his brother in a rolled up carpet.

Ok he told the men clean out the incinerator We are going to cremate Manola and take him home.

The interior of the incinerator was swept clean and Monola placed in.

Panzanala crossed himself and hit the red button the gas ignited with a whoosh and Manola was reduced to ashes these were gathered up and placed in a colored vase with a lid and the switched off and left.

The same day a resident reported a break-in at flat 27 and the police discovered Annie's body. The crime scene was very unusual as there was obviously been another body in the flat as there was blood on the couch the police were baffled.

But Charley had made a mistake one of the bullets he had used on Manola had gone through and through and stuck in the couch forensics found the bullet and checking records found it matched one in their data base.

Sarah Keo the Leeds Pathologist went to find Sargent Moffatt.

Hay Serge the bullet I found at the flat in Garforth matched one on the data base It came from a gun used in the Bikey murders in Wetherby a couple of years ago. Ok, Sarah said. Sergeant Moffatt better get in touch with Harrogate.

Meanwhile in Mexico Charley and Albert approached the outskirts of Campeche and stopped at a road house and booked in

In the bar they ordered a steak and chips each the waitress a young Mexican girl brought the steaks to their table. Thank you Charlie told her Your welcome sir she said.

What is your name? Charley asked. Alarma Sir. Ok Alarma tell me do you know the Sinolian Cartel. Alarma immediately spread over her face and she hurried away into the kitchens.

In a few minutes an elderly man came out of the kitchen and came up to the table. Good evening gentlemen I am Hugo Alarma is my daughter you are strangers here in Campeche and its very very dangerous to be asking about the Sinolian people They are not nice people and they have men everywhere.

Charley stood up and offered his hand Sir I am sorry if I scared your daughter but we are not what you think in fact it would be better if you forgot my question please.

He stared into Charlies eyes I can tell a good man when I see one he said the Cartels headquarters are about 3 miles further on this road on the left down Secumne road it's a huge complex but it's a very dangerous place please be careful many people have disappeared from around here.

Charley took him by the shoulders and shook him gently Thank you, Sir thank you very much please apologize to your daughter for me and please do not mention this conversation to anybody.

Good luck sir with whatever you have in mind. With that he turned and returned to the kitchen.

A man sitting at the next table got up and walked out Charley saw him and turned the man looked directly at Charley and went out.

Later in their room Charley said to Albert I think we were overheard in the bar tonight we have to be on guard I will take first watch.

This certainly wasn't Charlies first rodeo and he was alert and ready hidden in the bushes with a clear view of the cabin and the entry from the road.

At two thirty a black range rover pulled into the car park in front of the main building and two men got out both carried automatic weapons.

They walked towards the cabin no 25 they must have been told which room Charley and Albert were in. When their backs were turned Charley silently went to the side of the block hidden from the two men Charley had picked up a half brick their room was second from the end and as Charley carefully came round the block he was 2 meters from the nearest man he threw the half brick with force at the man's head it struck him and he fell into the other man as this man stumbled Albert came through the door and hit him squarely in the face he also fell.

Charley and Albert collected the guns and using ties they had bought on their way tied the two men finding spare magazines in the range rover.

Well Albert said Charley its three am let's give them a rev up.

At their last fuel fill up on the way here they had bought two jerry cans and filled them up with petrol they put them in the range rover the two men in the back they drove to Secumne street and turned up as they approached the estate a huge ornate gate across the entrance opened as they approached obviously the people inside recognized the vehicle and nobody even considered it may not be the two men from the cartel in the range rover.

As the range rover neared the complex it came to a stop Albert jumped out and rolled to a prone position in the grass at the side of the brick paved drive.

Charley put the automatic into drive and place a brick on the accelerator he then also rolled over onto the grass.

The ranger rover picked up speed towards the building it ran directly into the large glass windows of the huge lounge and crashed in. Charley had removed the caps to the jerry cans and as he rolled out tossed a lit match box into the well behind the driver's seat. Inside the building the range rover exploded sending burning petrol in showers into the lounge then bottles of spirts started exploding showering flames everywhere the whole main building suddenly in flames.

The shock of the attack was so swift it left staff and the other gang members disorientated.

Charley and Albert quickly made it to the wing on the left untouched for the moment by the fire luckily it was the armoury.

Parked in front was a Hummer they loaded in boxes of hand grenades' and automatic weapons Uzis AK 47's.

In the office at the rear Charley found 10 boxes they contained bundles of 100 dollar bills He grabbed a holdall from the office and loaded up the bag with about two hundred thousand dollars as they left they both pulled pins on two grenades' and tossed them into the armoury.

They drove out in the Hummer the armoury exploded in a huge number of explosions as the ammunitions ignited.

The whole complex was now in flames the sky was bright with the fire.

Satisfied with their efforts Charley and Albert stopped at the entrance and looked back at the holocaust. That's for you Annie said Charley.

As they still had the keys to their room at the red Coyote, Charley went into their room he opened the AC cover and placed the money in the ducting pushing it back so it could not be seen through the grill.

Panzanala's phone rang he picked it up a trembling voice spoke.

The whole estate is gone 12 people dead there is nothing left.

What how did this happen he roared The voice said two men came and did it. What two men We don't know we just know they asked in the red coyote where the cartels headquarters were we sent Carlos and Efundo at night to deal with them they sent them back in their range rover and burnt the complex down Carlo and Efundo we sent to deal with them were in the back burnt to death.

This was something absolutely outside Panzanala's comprehension he had built up his empire through fear and extreme violence but rarely had this kind of retaliation even the governments armed forces feared him.

This cannot be happening he thought Then his devious mind turned to who was behind this First his brother now his home complex he vowed to find out and take retribution.

Charley stopped at the red coyote and spoke to Hugo I have destroyed The Sinolia cartels complex he told Hugo but I haven't yet cut off the head of the snake they will know by now that you talked to me perhaps you should get your family out of the way for the time being but I can promise you I will finish this and cut off the head of the snake but it may take time. Again Hugo looked at Charley full in the eyes. You are a good man senior Thank you for the warning I will send my daughter to a safe place.

If you have trouble with the cartel, please ring me and he gave Hugo his phone number.

Charley and Albert drove Tuluca Where they set the Hummer on fire.

A taxi took them to the airport where they boarded a plane back to the UK. As they landed at Leeds and Manchester airport Panzanala's jet took off for Mexico. Before they left Panzanala had found a way to take his brother home.

The cartel had acquired a rundown abattoir off Rooley lane at a industrial complex in Bradford which they now operated as a pig abattoir it had an old incinerator to dispose of unwanted animal waste at two AM on Sunday Panzanala and his three men entered the building carrying his brother in a rolled up carpet.

Ok he told the men clean out the incinerator. We are going to cremate Manola and take him home.

The interior of the incinerator was swept clean and Monola placed in the circular drum.

Panzanala crossed himself and hit the red button the gas ignited with a whoosh and Manola was reduced to ashes these were gathered up and placed in a colored vase with a lid and the switched off and left.

One of the Sinolia cartels successes was the production of cocaine not until they started producing it had it been made in Mexico.

They obtained Coca plants from a Columbian cartel and started employing a retired Columbian Henreeco who had been involved in the production of cocaine in his native Columbia Panzanala's father Panzo had set up Henreeco in a house on his farm and with money persuaded him to start up the growing of Coca and extraction of cocaine from the leaves.

This had grown until they had millions of trees under cultivation and when Panzo died of cancer Panzanala took over with his mother Henrietta built up the largest drug cartel in Mexico.

They now had large open aired building producing Cocaine from the huge plantations of coca trees a laboratories cooking methamphetamines and substantial poppy fields producing Heroin a massive concern.

Each separate process had a manager a trusted dedicated and ruthless man without any empathy two of these were Mexican Josa and Heroe. The third was a German Irwin they had all been with Panzanala since his takeover from his father Panzo Each of these managers had a couple of heavies Panzanala had four personal guards that was the total in the cartel very unusual in Mexican drug cartels but Panzanala was paranoid about security and he thought the fewer people involved the less likelihood of treachery.

Charley awoke as his phone pinged it was Hugo. Hi he said who is that? It's me Hugo from Mexico. Oh hi said Charley are you in trouble. No not yet I have sent Amarlia to stay with her brother in Ciudad Juarex. Way up north on the US border. Ok, said Charley what can I do for you. One of the people coerced into working with the Cartel works on the business side of the cartel His name is Jonn he is very interested in Amarlia and told her before she left that your efforts had made a big difference to his thinking he thinks perhaps you are the way out of his involvement no one had ever dared to attack the cartel let alone damage it to the extent you did and I think if you are still interested in cutting of the head of the snake he could be persuaded to help providing it can be done without putting himself in harm's way. What do you think Mr. Charley?

Ok let me think about it and in the meantime see if you can get a clearer picture of what he could do I will ring you back on this no Charley added Bye for now.

Once again Charley sat in one of the old elm spindle backed chairs in Jimmy's kitchen gently swirling his glass of Laphroaig. The Smokey smell of the single malt from Islay strong in his nostrils. He took a sip of the smooth peat loaded whiskey.

Well James he said what do you think do I go all the way it's a huge commitment this is no ordinary. Bikey gang this cartel is enormous and very wealthy. If I do go all the way, I am going to need a great deal of help and planning.

I know Albert would be in. Can you remember the Mexican guy who joined us before the Feluga campaign? What was his name Josa? said Jimmy. I have his phone no in my book I think he went back to Mexico when we finally broke up and left the Howards. Ok Give him a ring see what he is up to now and Helen, Helen Potgyter The polish girl.

Christ she nearly beat me in my last sniper competition.

I have her contacts as well Jimmy said.

Ring her as well.

Helen Potgyter was working for Right up security in Leeds Helen was six foot tall 200 lbs. of female power, straw blond hair cut short, crooked white teeth and attitude.

Jimmy phoned her and although surprised she was delighted to meet in the Bay Horse in Wetherby the next day Josa was on a phone so Jimmy left a message for him to ring back.

Jimmy and Charley sat in the Snug as Helen walked in. She smiled showing her crooked white teeth. Hello, Sarg and Corp how nice to see you both what will you have to drink asked Jimmy A pint of John Smiths bitter please she replied sitting down next to Charley.

Well Charley this is nice it's been a while.

Hasn't it just replied Charley what Have you been up to since we left the Howards. Well I have got divorced and am working for a poncy pratt of a boss at Right Up its nothing very exciting acting as guards on various proxy jobs quite boring actually.

What are you two up to.

Oh a bit of this and that he told her.

Jimmy placed a pint in front of her Don't believe him he exclaimed. He's been back to Afghanistan on a private mission Done away with a Bikey gang, put a bent assistant commissioner of the Yorkshire constabulary and, a leads Crime boss in Jail and burnt down a major drug cartels compound in Mexico.

Jesus Charley she exclaimed and what ya going to do for an encore.

Well exclaimed Charley I have decided to put the cartel out of business completely. Are you interested He looked her square in her blue eyes its bloody dangerous.

What more dangerous than babysitting arseholes she exclaimed laughing.

Yes, love just a bit. Are you still up to the mark with a rifle I need a very reliable sniper.

You Bet she said I go to the range every month not lost any of it.

Well Helen the job would be in Mexico no back up at all against a very extensive and wealthy drug cartel I cannot promise rewards but anything we take off their operation I think would be enormous.

We have Albert Donkin and we are trying to get Josa the Mexican Oh yes I remember the Donk and the Beaner both good men Well I am in 100 percent Helen stated with conviction any operation with you Sarg is guaranteed successful. I haven't felt like this since we left the Howards.

Panzanala Stood in shock in front of his burnt out house his face was black and forbidding he was shaking with anger how can this happen. I want to know he shouted.

We have lost half a million us dollars in weapons and equipment and nearly two billion US in money and product.

I need to meet everybody at my mother's house tomorrow early in the morning.

At the villa De La Henrietta in Telchac Puerto 5 hard faced men sat around the huge timber table eating breakfast.

Josa, Heroe, Irwin, Panzanala and Jonn Mascale. Ok Started Panzanala we have suffered a very serious blow to our business and we need to get on top of it I fear these people are not what they appear at face value perhaps my brother sitting now on the side board may have under estimated them I will not.

If they return, which they may not we need to get notice they are in Mexico Jonn spread some money around at the airport.

Irwin you go to the Red Coyote and find what information you can extract from them there. I will get a bunch of mercenaries 'from soldier of fortune Josa contact Fernando and restock our armaments.

Later in the day Jonn entered the Red Coyote he was nervous speaking to the girl at the reception he said I need to see Hugo she said he is in the office and indicated the door John went in and closed the door Hugo was sat at the desk he was surprised to see Jonn. Hugo could see he was nervous and guessed the reason.

Trouble John he asked. Yes, very bad Jonn replied The German is coming to see you on Pazanala's orders to grill you on the English men who burnt their compound Jonn said Hugo these men are very experienced ex-military I have told Mr. Charley the leader you may be interested in helping destroy the cartel I am sure after what they did last time, they can do this. How is Amarlia? Ok replied Hugo away up north she is safe Good said John.

Are you in contact with the English man asked John Yes replied Hugo Ok said John tell them and he told Hugo what had transpired at the meeting in the morning.

Ok I will, said Hugo please now be careful John. I will Hugo thank you and he left. He had parked his car at the back and as he left he saw Irwin's blue Mustang pull into the front car park.

Josa pick up his phone Hi he said hi Josa Albert replied in his broad Yorkshire brogue There is only one person I know with an accent liker that it's the donk. It's been a long time Albert but it's good to hear from you.

How are ya travelling Josa Oh ok josa replied but it's a bit slow I am working with my dad on our cattle ranch slow and steady no ups no downs.

How are you Albert Josa asked.

Same replied Albert but with a few good ups I have teamed up with Charley Parker. Christ I well remember Golden bollocks exclaimed Josa What have you been doing.

We have just completed a black op in Afghanistan Christ that must have been a blast.

I certainly was full of adrenalin rushes replied Albert.

Do you fancy and adventure? Josa Albert asked.

Well it would depend replied Josa what's it all about?

Albert took a deep breath they badly need Josa.

Have you heard of the Sinolia Cartel asked Albert.

Everyone in Mexico has heard of them replied Josa. Why he asked.

I did hear that they suffered a fire at the leaders house they say another rising cartel carried it out.

Ha! Ha! laughed Albert it was Charley and me he said for a while there was silence then Josa exclaimed Fucking hell Albert what are you involved in.

Well Charley has got involved they killed a friend of his and you know Charley when he goes he goes like a bulldozer he executed Manola Panzanala's brother.

He has now decided to completely destroy the cartel it all started with a Ex Howard called John who had sank very low after leaving the force he was delivering a million dollars' worth of cocaine to a dealer when he was mugged and the drugs stolen. His grandma contacted Charley and he agreed to help John but the cartel killed her and that enraged Charley so he killed Manola and burned their head Quarters.

He has got the polslky Helen Potgyter to join us he is serious at doing this and we need you what do you think.

Wow that a big deal replied Josa the cartel is known for its extreme violence and is immensely powerful and very wealthy.

Well you know Charley, extreme violence and money and power never held any deterrent to Charley. He has made his mind up to destroy the cartel and nothing is going to stop him. I even think if we were not to join him he would go it alone.

Ok Said Josa I am in what's the plan.

Well our only contacts at the moment is a road house owner near the cartels burnt out headquarters and he has a member of the cartel ready to cooperate with us. But the owner of the roadhouse Hugo may be in trouble.

Do you remember Huey the Irish chopper pilot asked Josa I do reply Albert best pilot we ever flew with?

Well said Josa he grabbed a Huey the yanks left in Afghanistan stripped it down and shipped it here and rebuilt it he flies it now as a contract service.

Do you think he would be up for it asked Albert I am sure he would be he is the same larrikin he was in Afghanistan and he greatly respected Charley like everyone who served with him.

Meanwhile the front desk phone in Harrogate police station rang The desk Sargent Jim Belmont picked it up Good morning Harrogate police station how can I help.

Good morning sergeant its Sarah Keo here Leeds police pathologist. Can I speak to the Lead Detective on the Wetherby Bikie murders. Yes of course Jim replied. That would be Detective Inspector Oldfield, he is out at the moment I will get him to contact you when he come in. May I ask what this is about Jim asked.

Yes, Sarah replied we have a bullet here in Leeds which is a match for the one in the Bikie case. Right Harry will definitely be very interested. That case has bugged him for years.

At 3 pm Harry Oldfield came into the Harrogate station and read the note Jim had left on his desk.

He immediately rang the number on the note Hi Sarah Keo here Sarah answered. He said DI Oldfield I understand you would like to talk to me.

Yes, replied Sarah we have a bullet here in Leeds which is a match to one of yours in the bikie murders Christ exclaimed Harry Tell me the story.

Well replied Sarah We had a report of elderly lady not being seen for a while so when we investigated we found her diseased in her flat she had been murdered strangled so they sent forensics in to investigate. The situation then got strange we found blood on the settee and a bullet lodged in the arm the bullet matched one in the system involved in your case. Great said Harry have you matched the blood.

Now this is where it gets strange said Sarah We matched the DNA with a DNA on the FBI's international data base. Ok said Harry whose is it.

It is a senior member of the Mexican drug cartel Sinolia a man called Manola the brother of the leader of the cartel. But there was no indication of his body or whether he was killed or just injured.

Well said Harry if this is who I think it is he will be dead and he then told Sarah the history of Charley Parker.

Ok thank for this information I will let you know more shortly said Harry.

DI Oldfield's Blue Aldi pulled up in front of Charley's rose bushed filled garden. Charley stood up from his chair.

Good morning inspector Charley said what can I do for you this time.

Good morning Mr. Parker Harry said.

I would like to talk to you about an incident in Leeds a couple of weeks ago. What incident said Charley innocently. Harry a very experienced policeman knowing Charley hadn't really expected any reaction but he was a little disappointed at Charley's lack of reaction.

Charley however was surprised though he didn't show it how have they connected him to what happened in flat 28.

In a flat in Garforth near Leeds there was two murders harry said

Charley looked at him quizzically what has that to do with me he asked.

Please said Charley sit and he indicated the chair by the little table.

They sat down.

One of the murders in Leeds was Mrs. Longstaffe Well said charley her grandson is John Bailey Ah exclaimed Charley John Bailey eh.

Now I see how you have connected me I helped John to get clean he served with me in Afghanistan.

But that's not all Charley said Harry the other murder was a man called Manola Sinolia a member of the Sinolia drug cartel in Mexico.

Oh said Charley still without any surprise showing.

Yes, and the bullet the police think that killed him came from the same gun that killed two Bikey in the murders you were a suspect.

Oh said Charley again. Then he surprised Harry the police think it killed him don't they know Charley said.

Fuck me thought Harry this man is even better than I imagined.

Well that's where this case gets strange the pathologist could tell the blood was life blood so he was killed but the body wasn't there.

Oh Said Charley again still showing nothing.

You came here to tell me what asked Charley.

I came to see if you can shed any light on this mystery.

Well I am sorry I cannot have said Charley.

Well we have checked on your movements recently and noticed you went to Mexico and according to the Mexican police shortly after, the Sinolia's compound was destroyed.

Nothing to do with me Inspector Charley said.

Well Mr. Parker I really came to see you for a number of reasons one of which was to warn you if you are involved with this drug cartel the Mexican police told me they are the most dangerous people they have encountered.

Oh Charley laughed.

More dangerous than Hamdam El-fasi the bomber who made the bomb that killed 75 people in the Pakistan hotel bombing I shot him twice in the back of the head as he reached for the ignition switch to the 2 kg of semtex he had just primed or TicTac Mbobosa the Somalian war lord who's favorite pastime was chopping off children's arms at the shoulder with a Samaria sward he was two meters tall and weighed 200 kg I snapped his bull neck like a carrot and stuffed his severed penis in his mouth as a warning to his equally despicable army.

Or quiet O-Rourk the IRA bomber who killed 48 people in the Belfast pub bombing I gave him alive to the SAS who needed information he now sits drooling in a wheelchair in a Belfast care home.

These are some of the dangerous people I have dealt with.

I have done things and been to places so black that they cannot and should not ever be documented.

I have served my country and carried out black ops without question to the best of my ability.

Now I am retired!

Harry Oldfield climbed into his car he now had a different perception of Charley Parker and despite his 25 years of policing he could not help having a sneaky admiration for the man in the old green cardigan and brown corduroy trousers.

But the law was the law and he had also a sworn duty to uphold it and he knew Charley was involved just as he was also convinced he was behind the Bikie murders.

George Bentley despite his terrible history was allowed parole and his first day out of the juvenile remand center he was in the car park at Tesco he spotted Mrs. Thorpe pushing a shopping trolley towards her car a Toyota Corolla after she had loaded her groceries into the boot she got into the driver's seat and started the car as she started to move out of the parking space George walked in front and banged with his good arm on the bonnet Mrs. Thorpe braked and got out of her car oh my dear are you all right I am so sorry I didn't see you . George got up from his knees and as he stood up he pushed her violently and she fell hitting her head on the car park shade steel posts knocking her unconscious George walked to the open driver's side door and jumped in the keys were in the ignition and the motor running he put it into drive and drove out of the car park without giving Mrs. Thorpe a second thought.

Emilie Thorpe wife and mother of two girls Anne aged 8 and Celia aged 6 and husband Ray never regained consciousness and 4 weeks later her distraught husband agreed to halt her life support and it was turned off she was 38.

George parked Mrs. Thorpe's car 100meters down the road from Charley's caravan. He sat and waited patiently only leaving the car to pee and buy MacDonald's he wanted to get Charley in his car Before driving to Charley's house he called in at home he knew his older brother Ken had a sawn off shotgun hidden in the garage he grabbed it and a half box of SSG shells.

Back at Charley's with the shot gun on his knees covered by a paper both barrels containing a shot gun cartridge SSG cartridges have 18 extra-large shot in them used for large game such as geese and at short range lethal.

Charley pulled out of his drive as he did, he noticed the blue Toyota pull away from the kerb 100 meters down the road he noted it but it did not cause any alarm but as he turned onto the Knaresbourgh road he noticed the same car following now he was interested.

Charley pulled into a layby to see what the Toyota would do.

George now had to act quickly He drew alongside Charley's car and pointed the shotgun at the driver's side window but holding the shot gun with his one good hand was awkward as it was held in his left hand. The car now without a hand on the steering wheel hit a dip in the tarmac and the shot went over the top of Charley's car.

Charley saw the twin barrels so he knew there was still at least one shot left he had to be quick he slid across and jumped out of his car through the passenger door.

Quickly he went to the rear of the Toyota George was driving Holding the shotgun George was struggling to get out of the car Charley grabbed the barrels of the gun and pointed it away from him he pulled the gun towards himself and with his right hand he poked one finger into gorges eye.

George screamed and dropped the gun putting his good hand up to his injured eye.

Charley opened his hand and with the heel of his palm hit George just below his nose killing him instantly.

Luckily two of the SSG pellets had hit Charley's car which helped back up his story of being attacked. Once again DI harry Oldfield had to admit at least to himself Charley Parker was a remarkable man.

Sean Murphy (huey) and Josa sat in the bar of Maria's canteena and Josa relayed what Albert had told him what do you think Huey asked Josa are you up for a bit of an adventure You bet replied Sean It sounds exciting not a lot going on at the moment I am waiting for an army contract.

Did you bring any weapons out with you from Afghanistan At this Sean laughed two large boxes along with chopper parts, I haven't even opened he told Josa. Can we open the boxes and let Charley Know asked Josa. No probs Boyo replied Sean I will do it tonight.

What about you Josa you gunned up he asked. All I have is my father's 30-06 Josa told him.

Ok Sean let me know and I will inform Charley what you have in weapons and you are ready to rock and roll.

Hugo was sat in as chair in the bar his legs taped to the legs his arms taped to the chair arms Irwin stood in front of him with a pair of secateurs he had already cut of one of Hugo's thumbs. I want to know what you told the people who burned down our buildings he said menacingly n n-nothing said Hugo nothing they asked but I said. I didn't know he said Irwin placed his other thumb in the secateurs as he was about to cut off his other thumb he stopped as they all heard the wop, wop, wop of a helicopter.

In the large wooden crates in Seans workshop was an assortment of weapons 15 AK 47's 3 styre rifles a BarrettM82 50 Cal 12 assorted handguns 25 kg of sempex packed in 1 kg blocks and 3 hand held rocket launchers with 30 rockets and hundreds of rounds of ammunitions for all the weapons.

In another box was an assortment of flak jackets bullet proof vests and camouflage sniper's suits and netting.

Enough to start a war Charley told Josa when he phoned Charley.

Ok we arrive on flight BA326 on Monday next Can you meet us at the airport there will be myself, Potty and donk.

I will be there I have primed up Huey he is excited Josa told Charley as am I he added.

Ok see you next week bye for now.

Josa picked up the trio at the airport Mexican authorities very keen to have visitors so they passed through customs without mishaps'.

They arrived at Sean's compound 2 hours later and Charley briefed Sean on their mission.

We are going to completely destroy the Sinolian cartel he told them and as this is not a sanctioned deal we will take what we want from them. There will be no back up we are on our own so if anybody is fully aware of the risks and the danger there will be no repercussions if you wish to pull out.

There was no dissent.

Ok we will start off at the red coyote as I think that our friend Hugo will be in danger. How long is flight time to Campeche about 3 hours said Sean in Mexico there are very few regulations regarding aircraft so we should have no trouble getting there.

The old Huey with its brand new engine and rooters was loaded.

Helen drooled as she unpacked the brand new Barrett never been fired she breathed better test it she told Charley in the field at the back of Sean's compound they set up a target at 1000 meters a meter square white painted block board with a 50 mm clack dot in the centre the nearest house to Sean's compound was 3 miles away so the sound should not alarm people.

Helen set the tripod on a hay bale and got down behind the scope taking a fat brass shell she slid the bolt behind it and locked the bolt looking in the Leupold mark 5HD7-56 scope she picked up the target board she breathed out and in held it and gently squeezed the trigger boom the recoil pushed against her shoulder and 1 and a half seconds later the 360 gr tungsten bullet travelling at 4000ft/sec struck the board looking thought the spotters scope Charley said 150 mm high 250 mm to the right Helen took off the caps on the scope and turned the top one two clicks to the left and the bottom one 1 click to the right replaced the caps and slid another shell into the breech Boom spot on said Charley top quadrant in the black nice shooting Potty. She smiled want a go Sarg as she stood up.

No he said this mission you are the sniper. Anyway, not sure I could better that shot it was a great shot well done.

As he jumped from the Huey Charley said go Sean we will radio when we are ready no point putting the chopper in danger and the huey wheeled away.

Helen was spread eagled in the car park with Josa's 30-06 a man appeared carrying a AK 47 as he came out a 180gr bullet hit him square in the chest causing a hole between his shoulder blades the size of a tea cup at the same time Charley Josa and Albert burst thought the lounge doors striding over the downed dead gunman.

A very surprised Irwin turned from Hugo in shock as both the other two men fell dead to Alberts Glock. What the fuck he exclaimed but his voice died as Charley shot him in the right knee he fell to the floor. Clasping his shattered knee his mind now in a red mist when he came to his senses he was tied to the chair recently occupied by Hugo his leg ached and he groaned with the pain. They had pulled down his trousers and his heavy underpants his large circumcised penis exposed how will you cope without this monster the man holding it said ok yo he grunted Charley placed the secateurs at the base having difficulty getting the blades open enough to go around the large cock.

Ok Jerry I need to know where your drug operations are or you are going to lose this monster Irwin knew he was beaten this man meant what he said and he realized this man was behind the fire at Panzanala's house.

Ok ok he shouted.

Well said Charley slightly closing the secateurs no no please Irwin again pleaded.

Charley released the blades slightly.

The cocaine processing is just outside Peto The heroin is at Hopelchen.

Charley contacted Sean ok come pick us up please at the Red Coyote.

They dragged the dead men into the car park and placed Irwin in the chair with them.

Charley then phoned Panzanala.

Sean picked them up and they took Hugo to the local hospital

Ok said Charley lets go and have a look at the Peto operation.

Previously a letter appeared in Charley's letter box Hi picked up the pale cream envelope and turned it over on the back it read Peabody Harewood and Cronk.

Attorneys at law
Po box 375
Boroughbridge
North Yorkshire

Perplexed he opened the envelope.

The letter read.

Mr. Charles R Parker,

We are the solicitors for the late Betsie Harewood who sadly died 8 weeks ago we are the trustees of her last will and testament.

She left everything all her property and goods and chattels to you Mr. Charles R Parker my great nephew.

We have now wound up her estate which is 1,150000 pounds - 50 pence that money is now in our trust account.

Please inform us your bank details and we will transfer the aforesaid amount to you.

Yours sincerely,
Augustus Cronk LLB, Senior Partner

As they approached Peto They circled the small town outskirts the sinola establishment was easily identified by the acres of bright green coca plants and a large roofed building at the head of a small valley three old battered buses were parked nearby. they will be the transport of workers Sean said.

Ok said Charley we will have to attack this after they leave. Let's find a good place for you Helen and also a fallback position if they locate you flying low, they skirted the establishment keeping a safe distance. About 500 meters from the building was an escarpment from a higher plateaux landing on the high ground to plan their attack.

They found a suitable place for Helen with a clear view of the building well within the Barretts range.

And protected on three sides by a rocky outcrop and another hide behind bushes 300 meters to the right still with a good view of the buildings and a small path leading to the escarpment.

Examining the building through Seans binoculars with night vision capabilities they could see the drying tables and other cocaine paraphernalia there were about 50 women working in the shed there was also three men carrying automatic Uzis. At one end was a container converted into an office.

When they leave tonight we will get down there with some of that semtex and destroy the building but I want to get into that container first said Charley. He was also surprised that there were only three men as Panzanala must have found Irwin by now.

As they were setting up for the attack two black range rovers came into the compound and 6 men got out of each heavily armed and wearing combat gear hard looking men obviously ex-military

Ha! ha! exclaimed Charley as I expected Panzanala's private army. Tell Sean to get the chopper well away out of sight. Ok Helen get set up and target the leaders first. We will go down there and poke the wasp.

The three of them approached the compound in vee formation Charley leading as the got to the edge one of the mercenaries came out of the building he was a large raw boned bald man with an eagle tattooed on his neck. Hey numpty he grunted fuck off this is private property and he loosed a stream of shots to the side of Charley's feet. Without a flinch Charley raised his right hand there was a faint boom and the man's head exploded, as the bullet expanded, travelling at 4000 ft/sec.

Take cover Charley said.

As he said it the other mercenaries' started out of the building firing wildly the first one fell in a heap with a teacup sized hole in this chest armour as the boom of the Barratt died away.

Jeez Sarg Helen is the business said albert, spot on Albert replied Charley the best.

Charley shot the next man out and Albert the next two 5 down 3 to go plus the regular men oh oh breathed Charley as the Barratt spoke again 6 down.

One of Panzanal's men ran out of the building and ran towards the cars Charley raised his left hand.

The Barratt was silent they watched as he reached the first vehicle Let him go said Charley I need Panzanala to know what is happening.

Another two of Panzanal's men appeared at the door firing wildly in the general direction of Harley but the bullets going all over nobody hit Albert shot the one on the left as Charley raised his right hand the distant boom of the Barratt sounded as the second man fell. Ok Charley shouted you remaining two have 10 seconds to come out without weapons and you can leave with the remaining car. My problem is with the Sinolia cartel and I guess you are his hired guns no need to die for him as you will if you don't take this offer. On the top of the gable was a cockerel weather vane. Slowly turning in the breeze. Charley raised his right hand The head of the bird disappeared and it swung wildly. As the boom died away two men came out of the building with their hands raised up.

Jeez Sarg it's been a while the first man exclaimed.

Jimmy bloody Wilson Charley exclaimed. Is this how you spend your retirement sarg said Jimmy intimidating innocent Drug cartels. Charley laughed and you Jimmy risking your life defending them.

Sempa fi golden bollocks looks like the legends true eh. But who the fuck is your sniper Apart from you I only know one other that good. Its potty isn't it My god if I had known I wouldn't have taken this mission.

Look Sarg we have been paid for this exercise and I for one have had enough what about you George he looked at the second man Jimmy I will if you will.

Ok Sarg do you need help not really Jimmy I think we have done all right up to now but we would be stupid to refuse extra good men.

Ok said Charley lets sort this out they entered the shed and addressed the frightened women.

Can anybody speak English asked Charley the chatter stopped and an old lady wearing a white coat came forward I can sir she said. Right said Charley I am closing this operation down can any of you drive. Yes, sir she answered. Ok said Charley Get yourselves home on the busses.

After all the women left, they entered the office. Three large black holdalls were on the floor Charley opened one It was full of us dollars Josa get these into the chopper, contact Sean get him to land in the compound, the spoils of war he laughed.

They set 8 - 1kg blocks of semtex around the building with 30 min detonators ok said Charley lets go.

As they walked out the Huey landed in the compound. 10 minutes after they took off they heard the crump crump crump of the semtex.

Heroe reached Panzanala's new headquarters in his mother's house villa De La Henrietta.

The guard on the huge wrought iron gates let the black range rover in he drove up the opulent port cohere.

When he relayed the events at Peto Panzanala turned very white he was shaken badly.

I think the only way out of this mess boss Heroe said is to try and negotiate with this man I do not think you can beat him by force he appears to be very very good at what he is doing and he seems to have a great deal of military experience and well trained men. I don't think money will interest him there was 45 million in the office.

Yes, we are in trouble Heroe Panzanala told him Irwin gave him the address of the heroine plant. He will go there next.

At Hopelchen Charley and his growing army had no problems They killed the two men guarding the plant. The semtex again demolished the plant.

When news of this reached villa De La Henrietta Panzanala knew he was beaten the largest Mexican drug cartel was on its knees He ordered his Jet to fly to his villa in Nice.

The day after he left the Huey landed on the front lawn as Charley stepped off stood on the front porch was a tall elegant old lady leaning on a silver cane with two armed men one on each side.

I am not here to hurt you madam; said Charley and she gently touched the arms of her guards and they disappeared inside the opulent villa.

So she said softly so you are the person who has destroyed my son Panzanala and killed his brother Manola Both my sons and my husband were violent men and I suppose you could say they lived and died by the sword. But they were my blood. With that she pointed the silver cane at Charley and pulled the trigger the little 22 bullet struck Charley's Kevlar vest and it knocked him back a step She was surprised not realizing he was wearing a bullet proof vest. Well I cannot blame you Charley told her. I still intent to completely destroy your empire. At the gun shot the two guards rushed out tell them to stand down Charley told her unless you want to lose them Albert stood on the left Helen on the right with pistols cocked all Charley had to do was raise his right hand. Ok Boys do as he said she told them. Where is he Charley asked surely you don't expect me to tell you do you the lady replied.

Charley ignored her and walked into the villa in the opulent lounge on an antique table there was a number of photographs in silver frames one showed A large florid man with a bushy black moustache stood in front of a Lamborghini car behind the car was a French villa. Charley picked up the photo. Albert he said ask Josa to come here please. Josa please ask the staff where this is will you. Josa disappeared and returned in a few minutes it's the families villa in Nice he told Charley.

The old lady stood in the doorway Bastardo she said bastardo. Good day madam and with that Charley left.

A few weeks later in the extravagant pool area of the grand empire casino in Nice a large Mexican man with a bushy black moustache lounged beside the pool a young attractive waitress brought him a tall frosted glass with an orange colored cocktail a straw and a small pink umbrella your eastern sun rise sir she smiled brightly. The man eyed her skimpy waitress uniform and smiled thankyou he said.

He took the straw and umbrella out and dropped them on the table. He took a huge swig of the cocktail, the tequila masking the musky taste of almonds. 30 seconds later the man slumped in his chair with his mouth opening and closing clutching his throat 5 seconds later he was dead.

By this time the waitress had replaced her uniform in the changing room she had taken off the racks previously and was merrily walking along the boulevard Saint Eclair holding hands with her boyfriend Jonn walking slightly behind was an elderly man with one thumb.

The Red Coyote was sold to Emelio Devante and was being refurbished. The project manager noticed that the AC vent in cabin 28 had loose screws he told the builders to tighten them!

Milly Pearce had worked in banking virtually all her life her husband Ex Colonel Pearce had always encouraged his wife in her work Milly ended her working life and entered retirement. What few people knew was that Mill was the manager, before she retired of the overseas investment and banking arm of the giant banking concern Grouber Blackthorne handling huge amounts every day.

She had told Charley during their talks about her and her husband's problems.

Charley now had 45 million US dollars in the universal banco de Mexico and he need it moved.

He sat down with Milly in her little cottage as they sipped tea. Charley made no mention of where the money came from and Milly used to sums even larger never asked but she became very animated when she realized she could help him and repay him for his help.

Charley gave her the bank details in the Mexico account numbers etc. and his personal details.

I do not think you want this known Mr. Parker and I am not interested in any of the details. Better you don't know replied Charley.

Ok leave this with me when the bank opens on Monday I will start. I will open an account in The Cayman Islands and transfer the funds into it. From there you with be able to draw on the account.

Thankyou Charley said and he gave her a hug you are a sweetheart No she said I owe you big time my Parker I am pleased I can now repay you, mums the word eh Charley looked at the little old lady and smiled.

Josa received 9.31 million pounds. He had settled back on his father's cattle stud he bought six Texas long horn cows all in calf good job the calves aren't born with horns he though as he proudly looked at his cows the largest had a horn span of 2.6 meters.

Helen Potgyter (potty) received the same She bought a horse stud in Somerset from a deceased Rock stars estate Bobby Reo.

Behind the large horse stables was a 1000Meter rifle range.

Sean also received the same amount his contract with the Mexican army was renewed for another 5 years.

Sean bought another two helicopters and expanded his business

Albert Donkin received his share although he already knew it was coming he was shocked, as he looked at his account with the standard bank 9.31 million pounds seeing this amount in his meagre account, was somehow shocking.

Albert lived with his mother in a 2-bed terrace house in Beckwath ave in Grimsthorpe.

He was sat alone in the Red Ox with a pint of John Smiths Bitter. Pull yourself together Albert he thought. He finished the pint and left the pub.

Next day he told his boss Harry Rowbottom of Rowbottom bricklayers he wouldn't be back on site.

The next day he walked into Rawson and Turnbull real estate's office and bought a nice 3 bed new house in Dore. He moved his old mum in packed a few things in a backpack and left for Thailand on an open-ended ticket. For the first time in his life he felt satisfied.

Charley sat in Jimmies kitchen swirling the Laphoig in his glass. Well Jimmy we must come up with a new idea on the armoury. We can't leave them under the straw much longer.

In Villa De La Henrietta Maria Sinolia looked up sadly to the ornate sideboard at the two large vases she walked slowly out onto the large veranda and looked up at the stars.

She had sold the Coca plantations and the poppy fields to an up and coming young drug cartel. Liquidated the overseas houses and villas and the abattoir. The Sinolia Cartel was finished but the drug trade never dies other hands take over.

She walked back into the lounge and picked up the phone, opening a silver bound note book she flicked through the pages until she found the number she wanted.

She dialed the number. A voice mail "you know what to do leave a message". She paused a moment annoyed. Henriette Sinolia Ring me I have a contract I want carried out and she replaced the Alley Masoude was an extremely well trained respected member of Mosad Israel's secret service. He had undercover infiltrated a Palestinian terror group, unfortunately despite all his training and experience he was madly in love with a member of the group Lilly Patrube she through the Palestinian network was aware he was Mosad so she played him for all its was worth secretly garnering information. He should have been aware he was being played but his absolute infatuation blinded him to her careful information gathering.

She fed him information about a proposed suicide mission on the police station in Haifa when the target was actually the government offices in Jerusalem.

On Sat 25th July Lilly walked into the entrance of the government building and into the public foyer she was wearing a suicide vest with 2 kg of semtex standing at the reception desk she turned around and looked at the crowd's milling about.

She shouted Allah Akbar and blew herself and fifty others into oblivion.

At the enquiry although nothing was said about Allay's involvement He was devastated at his lack of intuition as he realized he had been played and such is human emotions he actually felt her death terribly so much so he decided to leave Mosad.

On Sunday morning three weeks after the explosion he drove to Jericho on the red sea here he stole a small aluminum boat and loaded two concrete blocks, an underwater powered hand submarine and his diving equipment and headed out into the red sea.

About 3 miles out he stopped hand cuffed his legs and fixed them with rope to the concrete blocks.

He took out his phone and videoed the boat and his tied legs and a panoramic view of his position.

Carefully avoiding the covered submarine and his diving gear.

He then sent the video with a note to Zeno Mamood the team leader explaining his involvement with Lilly Patrube and expressing his sorry at his lapse in dedication to Israel and to die was his only option.

He then unlocked his handcuffs put on his diving gear pulled the plug in the boat's bottom grabbed the powered submarine and jumped over the side treading water he watched the little boat slowly sink into the blue depths and headed for the shore.

Allay had parked his car someway away from the harbor carefully checking there were no security cameras covering the area. He landed on the shore close to where he had parked his car.

He quickly placed his gear and the submarine in the boot and dressed in jeans and tee shirt and made his way to the motel he had previously booked in. The green olive grove motel on the outskirts of Jericho. In his room he shaved his head and beard and put in blue contact lenses.

He then glued a scruffy blond wig on his newly shaved head and looked at himself in the mirror.

The image that stared back at him matched exactly the one in his UK passport Jimmy Liddle.

Stopping at a cheap car yard he did a deal with the salesman to trade in his Mercedes for a small Battered Toyota and pocketed fifty thousand five hundred Shekels. He then sold his gear to a second hand fishing tackle shop.

On the outskirts of Jerusalem at a scrap yard he paid the yard manager ten thousand Shekels to crush the battered Toyota and stood and watched as the cube of mangled car was dumped on the pile.

Catching an Uber, he arrived at Ben Gurion airport and Jimmy Liddle booked and paid for a one-way ticket to Mexico on El Al flight EL275.

All this took place 25 years earlier and Jimmy Liddle was now one of the most experienced hit man in the world he was known as the shadow nobody was aware of his physical appearance or his whereabouts he was only contactable on the dark web under his nick name the shadow. His regular customers had a burner phone number which was changed every month and customers referred back to the new number.

Talking to Henrietta in clipped tones he instructed her to meet him in Toluca next Thursday at 12:00 pm I will be in the café Reema on Pedro Boulevard bring the contract details as you know my fee is US $150.000.

On Thursday at 11.50 am Henrietta's black range rover parked a 100 meters down the road from café Reema driven by her driver Don he opened the door for her and followed her towards the café Jimmy was sitting at a table outside the café. She sat down opposite Jimmy. Don sat a few meters away. She placed a large heavy package on the table and slid it across to Jimmy.

Jimmy opened the envelope and looked inside he could see the money and quickly calculated that the amount was correct he had done business before with the Sinolia cartel. He took out the Photographs they were of a middle aged man tending a rose bush and a sheet of paper with an address in Knaresborough Yorkshire north of England.

Jimmy looked up at Henrietta quizzically. Are you sure this is worth you spending US $150.000 Don't be fooled by this man's appearance she told him You will need all your skills to complete this contract. This man killed both my sons and finished the Sinolia cartel he is the devil.

Jimmy looked again at the photos really on these he looks like an old grand dad, well Henrietta said don't be fooled he is dangerous. Ok I will make plans and they stood up Don and Henrietta left in the Range Rover and Jimmy watched them leave thoughtfully. He picked up the package and walked to his car.

Jimmy came up behind Charlie and looped the garrote around his neck but before he could tighten it Charlie reached behind his neck and grasped his two little fingers. He snapped them both one broke the bone the other was wrenched out of the socket tearing apart the tendons. The pain was tremendous Jimmy let out a roar but released the garrotte. Charlie whipped around with the speed of a striking snake and king hit Jimmy full on in the face Jimmy was gone in a burst of light, stars and then black. When he came too he was duct taped to a chair he slowly opened his eyes and Henrietts's words came back to him.

He was in an old farm barn on a chair in the middle of the large space at the end facing him he could see sheep in a coral. His little fingers ached his arms were taped to the chair arms he looked at his hands both his thumbs were sticking up and looked deliberate which he found strange but suddenly he remembered a similar situation during interrogation in his Mossad time and he shuddered.

Charlie came into the barn Jimmy turned his head to see him straining against the duct tape Charlie was caring a pair of secateurs'.

Charlie stood in front of Jimmy and looked down at him what is your name Jimmy Liddle.

Now your real name That is my real name he repeated Charlie bent down and placed the blade of the secateurs over his right thumb.

Charlie closed the blades and as the blades touched his thumb Alley Masoude he screamed.

Now we are getting somewhere. Who sent you Charlie asked

Henriette Sinolia Alley said.

www.ingramcontent.com/pod-product-compliance
Lightning Source LLC
LaVergne TN
LVHW010215070526
838199LV00062B/4588